OPEN
OPEN
Novel

Road
Book
Series

ML

Route 66 Déjá Vu

© Copyright Michael Lund 2023
Published by Glorybound Publishing, Camp Verde
SAN 256-4564
1st Edition
Published in the United States of America
ISBN   9798864602942
Copyright data is available on file.
Lund, Michael, 1945-
      Route 66 Déjá Vu/Michael Lund
      Includes biographical reference.
1. Adult Fiction   2. Historical Fiction
  I. Title

www.homeandabroadva.com
www.gloryboundpublishing.com

Route 66 Déjá Vu

We graduated in 1965 and were drafted

by Michael Lund

Glorybound Publishing
Camp Verde, Arizona USA
in the year 2023

Route 66 Déjà Vu

An abridged version of the novel was serialized on Kindle Vella in 2021. Revised portions of the following are included in the pages that follow: "Butt Dump," in *New Contexts 2*. London: Coverstory Books, 2021; "Bubba, Bubba, Bubba, Bubba." *The Review: Veterans Writing Project* (2018); "Old Soldier," in *On the Back of a Motorbike* (2016); "Left-Hearted," *Line of Advance* (2016); reprinted in *Our Best War Stories: An Anthology of Darron L. Wright Award Winners*, October 2020: Middle West Press); "The Voice of God" in *Eating With Veterans* (BeachHouse Books, 2015); "Boiling Lobster on the Fourth of July" in *How to Not Tell a War Story* (Milspeak Books and BeachHouse Books, 2012); *Miss Route 66* (BeachHouse Books, 2004).

Acknowledgements

Many people encouraged me in the writing of this novel, including Dr. Bud Banis of Science and Humanities Press in St. Louis, Sally Drumm and Tracy Crowe of Milspeak Books, and especially Sheri Hauser, the genius behind Glorybound Publishing. I learned from the accounts of Rolla high school classmates who served in Vietnam, including Larry Parks, Tom Batteen, and Bill Jenks. For encouragement to write I want to thank in particular Bernard Edelman, Elizabeth Mc-Gill, Geoff Orth, and William Frank. Jim Shifflett wisely edited an earlier version of this manuscript. Krista Gargano provided the cover design.

I'm grateful to many veterans and family members (especially Sarah Maddox Dunn) who've been involved with Home and Abroad the free writing program I direct at Longwood University. Other veterans Robert Partlow, Jerry Mebane, Valerie Orman provided insight into the rewards and costs of military service. With this book in particular I mourn Stephen Warner, killed in Vietnam; fellow Army correspondents who passed away recently, Tim McGovern. and Bernard Edelman; and Thomas Bragg from South Hill Virginia.

The book is dedicated to those who serve and those who care for them, especially Anne Lund.

Book Reviews

-- *"Route 66, with its endless stream of traffic and modest roadside motels and restaurants, provides the backdrop [to his stories]. . . . His characters move from their small stretch of Route 66 into the world beyond."--Nancy Beardsley,* Voice of America

-- *". . . was struck by how perfectly [the novel] seemed to encircle (of course) the world of childhood and its heady veering toward adulthood. It's a loving and funny book . . . and made me recall with mingled pleasure and embarrassment."-- Carrie Brown, author of* Lamb In Love *and* The Hatbox Baby

-- *"In Growing up on Route 66, Michael Lund gives us a loving look through the telescope of memory, resurrecting forgotten feelings in the idiom of adolescence sharpened by the lens of age--and wisdom. He takes us back to a time when the road ahead was a winding one, just right for joyrides, meant to be wandered, with curious roadside attractions and shady stops along the way. Reading [his] book is like returning to a summer night when you were young, when life was full of promise, mystery, and terror, that time at twilight, before your mother called you in to wash up and go to bed, when you were playing a leisurely game of kick-the-can and wished that the game could just go on and on. Fortunately, Lund promises that it will go on, in the second book in his series, Route 66 Kids, and, I hope, many more to come."--Eric Kraft, author of* The Personal History, Adventures, Experiences & Observations of Peter Leroy

-- *" . . . a howl with just enough of the serious to add contrast and spice."--William Hoffman, award-winning author of* God-fires, *and* Tidewater Blood

-- *"As an adult, the narrator has a philosophical outlook. 'The road I've traveled has clearer landmarks when I look behind me than when I was moving forward.'" Tricia Mosser,* Missouri Life

-- *"Lund presents an entertaining story of small-town life-paperboys, the gentle aspects of life in a simpler time and the wonder of the people who make small towns the linchpin of America. Through the eyes of Mark Landon we find that the answers to the myriad questions of life and love aren't always easy to find."--Bob Moore,* ROUTE 66 MAGAZINE

-- *"An extremely heartwarming and nostalgic look at young people's angst during this age of wonder."* ROUTE 66 FEDERATION NEWS

-- *"A wonderfully well-wrought novel, set in a place that's still the stuff of myth, about coming of age in a simpler time when sex was giddily mysterious and life was filled with endless possibilities." Bernard Edelman, editor of* Dear America: Letters Home from Vietnam *and* Centenarians: The Story of the 20th by the Americans Who Lived It

-- *"I highly recommend the stories in this book [*Eating with Veterans*] to all those drawn to serious writing about the Vietnam War and to seekers after the whole story—not just a narrow story told over and over again.—David Willson in Vietnam Veterans of America's "Books in Review"*

-- *"He has a rare gift as a storyteller. Many of the stories [in* How Not to Tell a War Story*] are written in a point-counterpoint method, alternating passages set in Vietnam with passages set back home after the war. This technique shows how inextricably linked the past is to the present and how a soldier's war experiences permeate an ex-soldier's later life. . . . Thanks to Michael Lund for bravely going with his short stories where no other Vietnam War author has gone before."—David Willson*

––––––––––––––––––––

Book One: Bill
Chapter One: Bridge

After the first high school reunion planning committee meeting ended in small-town Fairfield, Missouri, Curtis Lindbloom got in his rental car to drive back to St. Louis. But just as he inserted the ignition key, his classmate John Robinson opened the door on the passenger side and slid in beside him.

"Curtis," John said, "I'd like to do Janet. And I need your help."

Curtis tried not to show astonishment. Did he say what Curtis thought he said: "do" Janet? Janet was another member of the ad hoc committee organizing the event.

"Excuse me?" Curtis asked.

"I want to do Janet, and I need you to be my wing man."

"Do Janet?" Curtis asked again, pretending he still hadn't understood. He couldn't imagine Janet, a married, professional woman with grown children, entertaining a proposal of casual sex with a balding, pompous fellow 68-year-old.

"Yes," insisted John. "And I'm sure you know what I mean. We're both grown-ups here. She's still got a tight little body, and I never had a chance with her in high school."

"Okay, I do know what you mean. I don't see that I have any reason to help you."

John pulled his checkbook out of his coat pocket and

waved it in front of Curtis. "This is it. If you make the pitch for me, and she says yes, $5,000.00 goes to this scholarship fund you and Patrick are proposing. When the deed is done, another $5,000.00 will be added."

John's astonishment went up another jump. "That's a . . . pretty expensive . . . " He couldn't think of an appropriate word.

"Ride in the sack?" offered John. Curtis was grateful he used no cruder phrase. "It is, but I'm not paying directly for her favors. I'm contributing to a cause she believes in and hope she'll be . . . appropriately grateful."

"Yes, but is this a cause she would . . . " He wanted to say, "prostitute herself for"? But it seemed melodramatic for two seniors. "It's not a cause she would disregard her marriage for."

"In that case, there's no harm in your carrying the proposal to her. Janet can get back to me whenever she wants."

"I . . . I guess I can relay the message."

"Great. Tell her I can come up to St. Louis." Fairfield was roughly 100 miles west of the big city, where Janet was a fabric artist and university professor. "The Coral Court Motel, famous place along Route 66 for such liaisons in earlier days, is gone, alas; but there are other establishments in the downtown Arch area along the river for a more elegant rendezvous."

Curtis wondered if carrying on affairs in new upscale hotels rather than roadside motor courts was progress, regression, or standing still for romance in America. "I'll take your word for it." Feeling the topic had been exhausted, he put his key back in the ignition.

"Or she can come here," John continued, as if her acceptance was now assured, only timing and location to be worked out. "We could even, as we used to say, 'go all the way,' during the next committee meeting, if she'd prefer a return to one of our teenage places for such encounters. What's the point," he concluded, "of having arrived at this stage of our lives if it's not to do things we've always wanted to? Assuming we have the resources, of course."

Curtis shrugged and, when John stuck out his hand, shook it without thinking. He sat in his car and watched his classmate get in his Lexus. It occurred to him that he'd like to key that car.

A desire for sex or violence was far from the motive he'd had three months ago when he agreed to put together a reunion handbook with brief biographies, current addresses, and nostalgic photos from the original yearbook. He had idealistically imagined a bridging of divisions that had existed back then, a recognition of all that young people shared growing up in 1960s Middle America, and some consensus about what their children could hope for in the future.

Back then in their North Carolina river house, Curtis explained to his wife Beth. "I have proposed . . . " He paused for dramatic effect. "I have proposed a bridge party." It was a week before the first planning committee meeting was to be held.

She was puzzled. "And what's that? A party on a bridge somewhere, maybe at the Devil's Elbow where old Route 66 crossed the Big Piney River?"

Since he'd been working on a book about the Mother Road, that seemed to his wife a good guess. The bridge is famous because the road comes down a steep incline from the west, then bends sharply to reach the opposite shore. Historical preservationists wanted the old structure restored and preserved instead of being straightened out and made uninteresting.

"No, not a bridge across something, but the card game of bridge."

"The card game?"

"Exactly. I want to renew a half-century-old competition." He held out his iPhone to show the picture of a small house on a small lot. "That's Bill Castle's house in Fairfield on North Junction. Like a lot of old homes, it's been fixed up but looks very much the same as it did when I was a child."

"Okay, yes, a two-bedroom frame structure, like the one you grew up in. There were, as I remember, a number in the old neighborhoods, built as the town expanded in the 1940s and 50s, during and after the war. But why is this of interest?"

"Many Friday and Saturday nights, Bill and I played cards there with Susan and Cindy."

Beth asked, "You were couples, double dating?"

"No. None of us dated, each other or others—at least not much. We were the brainy, socially awkward kids who competed for top scores in every class. We could converse fluently in German but stammered through teenage small talk."

"So, you're going to use your mature rhetorical skills to persuade these three to play a few rubbers with you?"

"More than that. I'm going to find out who's living in the old Castle house—it's probably university students, since it's close to campus—and try to rent it for a night or two. Then I'm going to tell the old gang to come and play cards that weekend—in and around the other reunion events, of course.

How could they resist?"

All Beth could say was "Oh, my!" an expression she used more and more as her husband became caught up in reunion fever . . . among other late-life obsessions.

"There's one more thing," Curtis added. "I want Mom to come, too." Still sharp and active, his mother lived in a retirement home fifteen miles away. "The reunion coincides—roughly--with her 100th birthday, and I think she'll enjoy returning to the place where she and Dad raised three children."

Beth frowned but had to admit she was taking up some strange ideas herself in their retirement years. She'd been born "Anne Elizabeth" and went by "Anne" for most of her adult years. As a child she'd been "Beth." Now, wanting to recapture some aspects of her personality lost over the years, she decided to be "Beth" again and see how it suited her.

She knew her husband (always Curtis) enjoyed meeting old friends, perhaps because he'd left Missouri after college and lived his entire adult life elsewhere. He loved to tell the story of finding two classmates in a Cam Ranh Bay E-3 club on the other side of the globe. But she suspected his friends might have less enthusiasm for such encounters.

"So, seriously, you think you can lure your reluctant classmates to the reunion by recreating a . . . well, proposing . . . a goofy reenactment scene from yesteryear?"

"Ah, don't fool yourself: we all long for the innocent pleasures of youth! Shuffle, deal, play, repeat. That was our weekend recreation—with, of course, a little private fantasy by some of us thrown in, certainly by the boys. Now, of course, we'll add adult drinks and surround the table with tales of what we've seen and done over the past half century."

"Are you also inviting Kathryn Fahr?"

Curtis had always acknowledged he'd had a crush on Kathryn. Smart, lively, and physically attractive, she moved, however, in the upper social echelon of the school. He didn't play sports, didn't attend a church, and never acquired the necessary social skills to mount a campaign for her attention; so, he had admired, as he liked to say, "Fahr from afar."

"No, no. Different circle entirely."

Beth concluded, "Well, it's clear that, at the very least, you're going to get some good stories from this reunion."

He would, far more than he'd imagined. Of course, it's a time of life when folks have stories to tell. Some surprising tales even came out of his own mouth.

When he shook John Robinson's hand later that summer to end the discussion of "doing" Janet, he recalled how he had shaken the hand of the President of the United States after high school. He had told the story of that event many times. But he discovered in narrating the encounter to some class-mates that the better way to describe it was that Lyndon Johnson had grabbed his hand and never let it go.

Chapter Two: Centers

Curtis thought the girls would be harder to recruit for what Beth came to call—enjoying the redundancy—the "Castle House Project," or sometime just "CHP," as in "'chip' off the old block" (another pun, she would add, intended).

Susan Howe, Curtis knew, lived in California and proba-bly wasn't coming because of the distance (though she was a doctor and, one would think, had the means). He'd also learned from the chief reunion organizer, Barbara Lemon, that Cindy Martin had had an "undisclosed" incident with town officials some ten years ago and swore never to return to Fairfield.

Bill Castle had been a friend as well as bridge partner in high school, and Curtis believed the only real problem in recruiting him for the event would be locating him. According to Barbara, he'd dropped off the grid sometime in the '70s.

On the first trip to meet with the group planning the reunion in Fairfield, Curtis had the chance to see both of his siblings, which gave him more opportunity to explore the past.

Five years earlier, he'd begun the production of a family history. He recorded his mother's narration and then shaped it into a multi-volume saga. Her name was Marian Lacy Lindbloom, but she often went by the nickname of "Mid." They were revising the last book in the series in advance of a big birthday celebration when she reached a century in age. So, on this trip he checked some dates and facts with his siblings.

In addition, since bridge player Bill Castle had, for a brief time, been interested in Curtis' younger sister, Carol—though they never officially dated—he thought she might have some clues about where to look for him now.

Arriving mid-day on Thursday, Curtis spent the night at the house of his older brother, Louis, in St. Louis. The siblings and spouses relayed the successes (and a few failures) of their adult children living on four continents and in seven countries.

"I don't like to say they're 'far-flung,'" Louis insisted. "They all chose to travel to new places we never imaged going in our youth."

"I did a lot of imaginary travel as a boy in Chihuahua," noted Mark, Carol's husband. "But I was inspired by tales of the older people, not trips taken by anyone I knew in my village."

Louis' wife Suzanne, always the organizer, had put a magnetic flat pin (color coded for relationship) at each point on a large globe where one of the children—including nieces and nephews on her side—resided. Curtis and Beth's son Justin and wife were in Mexico, daughter Mary Anne in California, younger son Carl in Minnesota. Red pins spread wide.

With locating classmates on his mind, Curtis asked Carol and Louis, "Do either of you have any idea where Bill Castle is now? I've been 'volunteered' to do a Fairfield high school 50th reunion yearbook; and no one seems to know where he went."

Carol frowned. "When he dodged the draft, I was already in the Army. From that point on, we wouldn't have had much in common."

Louis observed, "I would guess he's in Canada or Sweden. If he were in this country—and alive—the electronic databases of our time would turn him up."

"I think about half of our class stayed in Missouri," said Curtis, "a fair number close to Fairfield. But some who became engineers at South Central State worked abroad. And those in the military—like you," he nodded at Carol, "were stationed all over the world."

She and Bill had been rebels in high school, but of opposing types. He mocked what he saw as Fairfield's narrow adherence to convention. He'd even petitioned student government for the removal of the "under God" phrase from the Pledge of Allegiance. And he argued with the girls that saving their virginity for marriage meant they saw their bodies as property, for sale.

Carol, a math prodigy, had been precocious academically. And, despite the concerns of her parents, she dated men at Central Missouri State in Fairfield. Late in her senior year, she shocked family and friends by joining the military, staying in for twenty years.

Bill's trajectory from high school did not match anyone's in his class. It would turn out that about two-thirds of his male classmates would serve in the military, a good number of them in Vietnam. It was their generation's war as young men. Civil rights movements would come to define their adulthood. Many, especially those who stayed in or returned to the Midwest, tended to be intensely patriotic and politically conservative.

"Let me tell you one story about Bill," Carol offered. "Maybe as a literary scholar, you can read it and predict the future he followed."

"I'm guessing it will be colorful."

She raised her eyebrows to suggest he didn't suspect the half of it. When she was done, Curtis would wonder if he shouldn't be working to keep Bill away from the reunion rather than encouraging him to attend.

"Do you remember his science fair project?" she began. "The sewer one?"

"Vaguely. Something involving mapping the town's system?"

"Yes. The advertised goal was to show how every part of the town was connected—Shoe Factory Addition, Fairfield Acres, Ridgeview (including The Circle, our neighborhood), even the cemetery. He drew a large black-and-white map, with the sewer lines beneath the roads and building outlines marked in red."

"I guess that would make sense. We generally think of streets as the network that organizes a community physically, but there are also drainage ditches, telephone and power lines, the town water system. They all lie above the sewer lines, which is a kind of underground digestion system—well, the final phases of it."

"But Bill told me," explained Carol, "that his project was not really about organizing all the houses, businesses, and people of Fairfield inside these grids. He said his project represented—to those in the know—draining stupidity out of the community. 'Flush it into all the toilets,' he laughed, tracing a route with this finger. 'Down the pipes, off to some purification plant. Maybe we can distill a tiny grain of sense from the town's collective wisdom.'"

Suzanne said, "Well, I never knew him, but he doesn't sound like a happy man."

Carol nodded. "He did have—or wanted to have—his pleasures. One Saturday night after a bunch of us were having milkshakes at the Maid Rite, he gave me a ride home. And that's where the colorful part of the story comes in."

"Is it suitable for young people?" joked Curtis.

"You'll have to judge. On the way through downtown he stopped at Main and Ninth Street, which he claimed was the exact geographical center of Fairfield. He even said, 'I know the single brick here that is equidistant from the town limits north, south, east, west.'"

Curtis winked at Suzanne. "Small talk for geeks, I guess."

"An aside," noted Louis. "In 2000 the geographical midpoint of the United States population was in Phipps County, about 20 miles south of the house we grew up in."

Curtis laughed. "I always felt I was the center of the nation, if not the universe."

"That's not odd. Most of the men I know think they're the center of the universe," quipped Carol. "Not you, of course," she smiled at her husband.

"So," Curtis asked, "had your friend determined the center of town just as a curiosity? Or was there a point to his showing you?"

Carol nodded. "I didn't understand it at first, but he went on to say it wasn't the heart of town he was interested in, but the hub of the town's sewage system. And that, he claimed, had to be figured in terms of elevation as well as surface distance."

Curtis noted. "Yes, it's a three-dimensional grid—X, Y, and Z axis—though why one would need to know that isn't clear to me."

Carol smiled. "You do know about cherry bombs in toilets?"

"Uh-oh," warned Suzanne. "It was a bad prank in those days, dropping a lit one down a toilet. The fuse burns internally and is not put out by water. When it goes off, you spray whatever's in the bowl all over the bathroom."

"If," cautioned Louis, "the fuse isn't too long. Some will explode farther down in the drainpipe and do serious damage." Seeing Suzanne's eyes widen, he added "Not that I ever had anything to do with such a prank!"

Curtis asked Carol, "I hope he wasn't going to blow up the town sewer system. I know he was an angry guy in high school and could have thought an eruption of sewage suitable revenge for 'brainwashing.'" He put the word in finger quotes. "Brainwashing all our young minds."

"No," she laughed. "I don't think so. That particular night he had another system he was more interested in." She waved a hand across her midsection and smiled.

That a teenage boy would be curious about the navel and other parts of a girl's anatomy didn't surprise Curtis. But the idea of explosives in the sewer . . . ? If Bill Castle had been thinking like that then, what—assuming he was still alive— might he be contemplating now?

"Frankly," Carol concluded, "now that I think about it, Bill Castle's past reminds me of some of the case histories I've read recently of what we call 'home grown terrorists.'"

Chapter Three: Subgroups

After lunch the next day, Curtis drove down from St. Louis to Fairfield and checked in at The Midwest Mother Road Motel, recently renovated as part of the National Park Service's Historical Route 66 Corridor Preservation Program. Fortunately, the decorations—pictures of old gas stations, diners, and other roadside attractions—were not overdone.

The members of the ad hoc reunion planning committee were to meet informally that evening at The Table, a popular Fairfield pizza place. The next day they would get together at John Robinson's house to establish an initial outline of events for the big weekend. One of Curtis' primary objectives tonight was to press Barbara Lemon for information about Bill Castle.

He had trouble getting her attention, though, as she was busy recognizing and finding places for arriving classmates among the Table's growing happy-hour crowd. Some were local, as was she, so it made sense she could spot them. More impressive was how she identified the out-of-towners, introduced them to those they wouldn't recognize, and knew who they would be comfortable with. She also provided an appropriate variety of pizzas and sent slices down the long table as if she were a blackjack dealer at a Las Vegas casino.

Barbara was, Curtis realized, clearly the person who should be editor of the reunion yearbook! And yet he had been dealt those cards.

When he'd accepted the job, he had only the vaguest idea of how material should be arranged. Should he copy the order of the original Confluence; include only those who responded to the mailing with a brief biography; use old photos and/or new ones?

After a time, Barbara sat down by Curtis and reported that she'd identified three more deceased members of the class and wanted to give him copies of their obituaries.

"This isn't good news," he admitted. "But I must say you're an amazing researcher. I wish today's college students were so savvy."

"Facebook makes this task easy," she laughed. "But learning about those we've lost," she gestured at the paper she'd given him, "does make it depressing at the same time."

"How many of our nearly seventy-year-olds are no longer with us?"

"It's in the area of 20 percent, I fear. Now, in terms of how many might attend the reunion, we're not counting those with serious health problems who are unlikely to attend."

Curtis saw his opportunity. "Say, have you found Bill Castle? Your last list had him in 'parts unknown.'"

"All I've learned—and that was some years ago—is too much drugs in the '60s, a few especially bad acid trips. He's not been seen by anyone around here for decades."

Janet Weaver, the artist from St. Louis sitting beside Curtis, asked, "Didn't he have an older brother? Last I heard he was still president of one of the Fairfield banks."

Barbara shrugged, which Curtis thought a bit odd. If the brother was here, why hadn't she at least given him a call?

When Barbara rose to greet someone across the room, apparently not from their class, Curtis tapped a memo on his phone to check about an older Castle. He would consult the phone books they still placed in motel room desks, though the primary function of such furniture these days was to hold up laptop computers.

As discussion down and across the table grew more boisterous, Janet leaned close to Curtis and asked, "Did you read Patrick's letter, about the scholarship idea?"

Curtis smiled. "Sure did. I like it."

Patrick, still practicing law in Austin, Texas, kept close ties with many in the class. Although he was not involved in the official planning for the reunion, he was ready to help. His letter said in part: "I propose that the class make the reunion a kind of fund-raiser. Rather than purchase a bench with a plaque on it, we could create a scholarship that would help send one of this year's seniors to college. Given the costs of schools these days, it could help."

Glancing around, Janet said softly, "Yes. But it may be a hard sell."

"Oh? Why?" Curtis had intended to support the idea wholeheartedly the next day. Thinking of how Beth accused him of indulging in nostalgia, he wanted to be able to site this project as a gesture toward the future.

"Just go slow and watch reactions."

Then a hand clamped down on Curtis' shoulder, and he looked up to see big Timothy Carlson, the basketball team center. "Curtis!" he exclaimed. "Good to see you. Come with me."

"What now?" thought Curtis.

This informal meeting was even less structured than he'd hoped. He had wanted to gather more input on ways to shape the yearbook. But Janet gestured he should go with Tim, so he followed to another table of men plus one woman.

"This is a subcommittee of the whole," explained Tim. "The Vietnam vets. You remember Mark, Gary, Jimmy—he's the damn mayor now!—Lonnie, and—last but definitely not least—lovely Sandra."

They all smiled a greeting, including Sandra, but, while brushing her hair back over an ear, she also discretely extended a middle finger in Tim's direction. "Tim, you flatterer. I'm not last, least, or lovely."

Curtis suspected she was farther along a road of women's liberation than some in her generation. And, he noted to himself, she was lovely.

"Good to see you," he told the group, shaking hands. He took the extra chair Tim borrowed from the next table. "I suspect there are quite a few of us in this category. You know, I'm going to be putting together . . ."

As he encouraged these vets to get their photo plus brief bio to him early, he added a mental note about a possible method of organizing the yearbook. He was going to send a sample entry about himself as a model. And he might add some sort of symbol for military service. There might be similar ways of highlighting connections: educators, business, civil service, agriculture, and so on.

Their generation had more varied options than had their parents in terms of lifestyle as well as profession. But he didn't think he could map the divorces, second marriages, combined families, singles, closet gays, or same-sex relationships that threaded through the class. Bill Castle's high school project of drawing up the sewer lines was simpler by far.

Mayor Jim was a key figure in the reunion group. After four years of ROTC at South Central State he'd served a year in Vietnam. He came home bitter about the limitations politicians imposed on the military and the relentless pressure generated by the anti-war movement. He'd buried his anger in hard work and service to his community.

Curtis hadn't thought about it until the last few years, but enlisting—or being drafted—had opened up his generation to the experience of other cultures around the world and subsequently determined in part how they shaped the future.

He'd gotten an itch to see distant lands from reading adventure tales as a boy. Half a mile into the woods on the edge of the neighborhood of his youth was a view west down to the Gasconade River, more than ten miles away. And snaking toward that location was Route 66. It underscored a path to the fabled West—Texas, New Mexico, California, and more exotic locations beyond.

His era's symbol of travel to the faraway, Route 66, passed only a few blocks from the house of his childhood. He'd never dreamed that the "distant land" he would visit was in Southeast Asia. And that trip was by air, not car. Even there he retained, at a cost, an innocence carried over from childhood—a belief in a simple order of people and events, a knowable system of interaction and communication to which he always returned for stability.

Along the route of "America's Main Street" had been souvenir shops, restaurants, and motels like the Midwest Mother Road Motel that catered to cross-country travelers with a crude portrayal of locals. He noted one of the more famous shops, Hillbilly Shed, as he returned from the Table that night. It was right next to the Mother Road.

Both establishments were located on another stretch of that ridge on the edge of Fairfield, but farther south and west from his childhood stomping grounds. Mine Road, near his motel, led down to another memorable landmark outside of what they'd always called "The Circle."

"I've got an idea," he told Beth that night over the phone. "An extra excursion after tomorrow's afternoon session."

"Does it involve Kathryn Fahr?" she asked with a chuckle.

"Alas, no. This will be a solo journey into one my old stomping grounds."

He ignored the groan coming from the other end of the line.

Chapter Four: Scholarship

Gray-haired, well-dressed Jackson Castle received Curtis in an elegant second floor corner office of Fairfield City Bank accessible by private elevator. He rose from behind a massive mahogany desk, stepped across fine carpet to shake hands and ushered his visitor to one of the two upholstered chairs (not the French-styled settee by the windows).

Curtis explained briefly why he wanted to contact, if he could, this man's younger brother. "A group of us are planning our class's 50th reunion—it's two years from now, we know. But we're trying to make sure all our classmates know early enough to 'save the date.'"

Jackson moved a memo pad in front of him but made no notes. "I see. Are you soliciting support from local businesses? Or would you like to establish an account here through which you can take in contributions and pay for services?"

Curtis hadn't thought about such things at all, but he did vaguely recall Barbara saying some of the local people had volunteered to handle expenses and logistics. "No," he said. "I'm not in on that end, but I've agreed to assemble a new edition of *Confluence*, a yearbook about the class. And, well, I wanted to ask you about Bill, where he is, and so forth, since he is one of us. Not just for the reunion, but I'd like to be back in touch for myself."

"Oh. You were one of his friends? You see, I am almost ten years older than he, so by the time you guys were in high school I'd been off to college and was working in Springfield."

Again, he shifted the memo pad, perhaps made a check mark on the top sheet.

"Um, do you have a current address?" Curtis asked. "Or phone number? Email? I know not everyone is on Facebook, and, if they've been elsewhere for a number of years, it's hard to know how to contact them."

"Um-hm. I see."

Curtis decided to wait for Jackson to volunteer whatever he would. The banker glanced over to the big window that looked across Main Street. "I . . . I sometimes take mail for him, or messages and pass them on. If you'd care to jot down your . . . what you're doing and your contact information, I'll see if I can get that to him."

Curtis concluded that Bill's whereabouts must be some kind of family secret. It did seem, though, that he was at least alive, perhaps living overseas, or the victim of some sort of illness—could be mental—or maybe he was just reclusive.

Jackson took the piece of paper with Curtis' name, contact information, and a note about the reunion. If Bill got in touch, Curtis would go into his scheme of bridge with the old gang.

"I assume you don't live in the home I visited so many times, over on Junction Street, a few blocks north of the university campus?"

He chuckled. "Oh, no." He gestured to the picture of an expansive brick home, as solid and prosperous looking as his bank. "But I do still own the building. We rent to students. It's such a convenient location, and it wouldn't be worth much if I decided to sell."

"Of course. Well, thank you. I'll leave it up to Bill to contact me. But please tell him it's more than a gesture. I'd really like to see him, talk about what we've done in the many years since we went away to college."

Jackson ushered him to the elevator cordially. When he stepped out, Jackson's secretary pointed him toward the teller area and the front doors beyond. Curtis was pretty sure Jackson would not press his younger brother about the reunion, but he had at least confirmed that Bill was alive and might respond to the call.

Later in the morning he found his progress on the scholarship idea was gaining no more success that his scheme to enact a card game from fifty years ago.

When he'd received Patrick's letter the previous week, Curtis thought it was a fine idea. The other members were copied, and he assumed most would respond positively. But reading the faces of his fellow organizers, he saw it wasn't going to be that simple. He made his initial plea with a reference to his own experience in Virginia.

"I went to this fundraiser back home a couple of weeks ago. We're trying to establish a civil rights museum in our town. You see, at the same time all of us started high school in Fairfield, the schools in the Virginia county where I lived for 35 years closed to avoid integration, part of the South's Massive Resistance. I've come to realize that we," he waved a hand around the assembled group, "we were a fortunate generation growing up in a generous community. We can show we recognize that with this scholarship fund."

He noticed that two or three of the ten looked down at the yellow notebooks that had been donated by Barbara's prosperous real estate business. The others were expressionless. So, he decided to fill in a bit more.

"Please don't think we're a backward Southern community, but I have witnessed the effects of an unfair social system carried forward to later generations. When my children went to school, some of their classmates had parents whose education had stopped at the fourth, fifth, or sixth grade because of the school closing. My three had educated parents who could help with any homework. But a lot had to be done to assist others in the next generation. And that's what we would be doing with a scholarship. A graduate of the class 50 years after ours could get a nice boost toward a college or vocational training."

John Robinson nodded. "You know, it would be just one student. And there are lots of programs now that assist the . . . assist struggling families."

"Yes," agreed Carol Yates brightly. "Things are so much better now. And what we want to do for our classmates is . . . is to give them a good time, to celebrate how much we've accomplished. A scholarship drive would . . . or, well, it might detract from the event."

Curtis tried not to show his disappointment. "Okay, but I don't see why we can't do more than one thing. As you know, I've been a college teacher for some years, and I see what small gestures can do for individual students. My wife and some of her cousins started a scholarship in memory of her grandparents, who lived in Rural. It goes every year to a graduate of the local public school to attend the university where I used to teach."

He saw again a few slight nods, but more unresponsive faces. "We're often invited to the scholarship award ceremony," he added. "And even though this person is only receiving a few thousand dollars, they are always so grateful."

Barbara Lemon smiled and said, "Well, we've heard now from you and Patrick, so I suggest we all think about this and see if we can find a . . . a resolution by the time of the afternoon meeting. After all, we have a lot else to discuss: the banquet, the band, housing, and so forth." She turned over the top page in her notebook and called on John to present his ideas on a dance and the theme.

Curtis retreated into the silent observer role he'd perfected in many faculty meetings. When John Robinson later asked his help in "doing Janet," he recalled how he, Barbara, and Carol had used their roles to artfully bury the scholarship idea. There was a pattern here.

During the lunch break, catered by a local restaurant, he caught Janet Weaver's eye and nodded to a quiet place on one side of the room. "Any ideas?" he asked her.

She shrugged. "About the scholarship? Sorry, not really. But talk with Gary, if you get the chance. He's involved in charity fundraising."

She explained that he'd retired a few years ago after many years in a prominent public relations firm and begun working for a local chapter of Wounded Warriors. He might, she suggested, have ideas on how to make the pitch.

"Duly noted. By the way, someone told me you were a 'textile artist,' and I have to confess I have no idea what that means."

"It's an ancient art, really. We use fibers—plant, animal, synthetic—to create both practical and aesthetic objects."

"Ah," he smiled. "You're a weaver!"

"Yes," she chuckled. "Destiny by name. I have my own studio but I teach also. So, we're not that different. You bring together words into lectures, essays, and books just as I create scarfs, hangings, tapestry. I'm sure your new edition of *Confluence* is going to weave all our life stories into one beautifully shaped history."

"Ah! Way to put the pressure on me. I was pretty much planning on a modestly annotated address book."

She cocked her head, "You know, perhaps you can use your solicitation of material as a sneaky way to promote the scholarship idea."

"Hmm. It could have a sub-text, like subliminal advertising at the movie theater. Instead of 'you're thirsty; buy a drink,' the message will be 'help a young person; give money.'"

Chapter Five: Side Streets

Curtis got the chance to talk with Gary late in the afternoon as the group enjoyed a break in the expansive three-season sunroom that looked out over ten acres of Missouri countryside.

He pulled two beers out of the cooler and offered one to Gary, a prelude to asking his help on the scholarship. But, as he was to learn repeatedly in this venture, his classmates, like so many at this time of life, had their own stories to tell that would take precedence over Curtis' interest.

Accepting the beer, Gary asked, "You remember the Old Soldiers Home in St. James?" The little town was a dozen miles east of Fairfield.

"Sure. Red stone structure on the east edge of town, visible from Route 66 though not from Interstate 44, which runs a few miles north."

Gary sipped his beer. "Never thought I'd be one. You know, an old soldier."

"I suppose, but we're finding these days that we're linked to groups we didn't see ourselves as part of in the past."

Curtis didn't mention the mental pictures he'd had as a child of the Missouri Old Soldiers' Home: aging pensioners, broken, bent, drooling figures mumbling about long ago wartime experiences. He didn't see himself like that—yet.

Gary sighed. "I'm struggling with what links me to my own past. You in 'Nam?"

"Yes. But I generally think of residents of the Old Soldiers Home as career military, men who spent their entire lives in that capacity. I was in just two years. That's why I like Patrick's idea of a scholarship; it makes a connection going forward as well as recognizing those of the past—us getting more education, them doing the same."

Gary took another reflective sip. "Ever want to go back? See where you were stationed?"

"No, can't say that I do."

Curtis realized that they'd turned their backs to the others, looking out at the fields.

Gary said he didn't know why he decided to travel to Vietnam forty-five years after he'd left. Just to see, perhaps. Or for closure. In a more philosophical frame, maybe he wanted to see a new country, post-American—or the old one, pre-American.

"But, you know, Curtis, it probably has as much to do with the discovery that I was an 'old soldier.' I'm not sure I ever accepted the fact that I'd been a young one. I had some crazy idea that I'd find my younger self there." He chuckled wistfully.

The Vietnam veterans Curtis knew, especially the draftees, thought of themselves as soldiers only for the time of their enlistment. Many had never anticipated a military career and returned quickly to their civilian lives—the lucky ones, of course.

"Where did you do R & R?" Gary asked.

"Sydney. Great time."

Curtis was having trouble switching the conversation back to the scholarship. He was also beginning to see that he would need to set very strict limits on each classmate's personal statement in the yearbook— "no longer than . . ."; "no political or religious pronouncements . . ." ; "professional and personal information . . ."

"I stayed in-country, Vung Tau, former French resort town," continued Gary. "Had an old friend stationed at a language school there. Got to spend a couple of days with him, but doing what, I don't remember now."

Curtis had enjoyed people-watching in Vietnam. City streets were full of young girls in white áo dàis on their way to and from Catholic schools. Street vendors hawked fish, meat, and vegetables. Laborers carried bricks or sand or water in buckets at the ends of shoulder yokes. Women walked with laundry stacked high above their heads.

He also remembered how some viewed such scenes as opportunities. The photographer he worked with would say, "That guy right there,' nudging him with an elbow. "I bet he's got good dope in his pack. He probably pimps for a whorehouse nearby. And he'll sell you a Rolex."

Gary got up and brought back two more beers. "I'll never forget one thing . . . one thing that happened in Vung Tau."

Curtis wondered if he should stop him. He'd learned in recent years some vets couldn't keep themselves from retelling certain events, their past on a video loop.

Gary went on anyway. "One night I'd had too much to drink the night before and didn't want to walk back to my hotel in the morning. So, this girl . . . girl I'd been with . . . she said, 'I take you, Mr. Soldier,' and pulled me by my elbow to a moped parked close. 'Get on behind ,' she said."

Gary turned to Curtis, "You ever ride one over there?"

"Can't say that I did." They were, though, a familiar sight.

Gary nodded, took another sip. "Well, hell, I just swung a leg over and put my arms around her waist. But I did ask, 'You good driver?'"

"She laughed. 'Sure thing, G.I.,' and revved the engine. Now, I'm telling you . . ." He glanced around to be sure no one else was listening. "That seat was already warm between my legs, you know what I mean?"

Glancing around, Curtis saw that everyone else sensed this was a private exchange.

Gary resumed, "The girl turned the handlebar and was starting to pull into the street when I felt someone climb onto the bike behind me, arms tight around my chest. I jumped—if you can jump straddling a motor bike! And this other voice behind me said, 'It's okay, G.I., okay. I need ride, too.' Man, I can hear that voice now!"

Curtis could too, the rhythm and tone of that musical language had stayed with him.

Gary and his two new friends pulled out from the curb, weaving through traffic, and headed away from the beach and his hotel. He said, "I shouted into her hair, 'Where're you going?' I'd heard stories of American soldiers delivered to the enemy by Vietnamese prostitutes."

"The driver turned her head slightly to the side so I could hear. 'Take girl to the doctor. Must have check-up every week. Everything fine, no worry.'"

Gary laughed. "The girl behind me said, 'Broad shoulders. You big man, Troop.' I could feel her lips on my ear!"

Curtis decided Gary had to go on to an end, whatever end that might be.

"It was like watching an action movie too close to the screen—images of buildings, vehicles, pedestrians streaming past. The only good thing was that it was unlikely I'd fall off, squeezed between these two women like we were in a New York subway car."

"Traffic in Saigon was crazy," Curtis admitted. "Indy car drivers were at the wheels—uh, at the handlebar—of the rickshaws."

"We stopped at a pharmacy," said Gary. "And the girl behind me hopped off, went in a door on the side of the building. The driver leaned back. 'One minute, G.I. Then my turn.'"

Curtis understood. "In a time of war, there's still a certain order. Soldiers, prostitutes, pimps who make sure business continues."

"You got that right. After a few moments, the first girl emerged, and the driver went in. Rather than sit behind, though, the second girl swung a leg in front of me, straddling the seat. When the first driver same out, she climbed up behind me. I was the meat in a sandwich again!"

"Just a lucky customer."

Gary admitted. "I felt people were staring at the tall American who didn't know where his hands should be. But the girls delivered me safely to Lotus House, by now, more or less sober. One said to me, 'You come to House of Saigon Sisters tomorrow.'"

Gary made sure only Curtis would hear him. "Then she said, 'you have us both, okay?'"

Curtis nodded. "These experiences stick with us."

"You know why this one does? A week after I got back to

my unit, I learned that my friend at the Vung Tau language school had bought it. He'd stopped to help a Vietnamese woman pulling a wagon full of shit to be burned."

He finished the last of his beer and crushed the can in his hand. "Shit, man! She was VC, and cut him down with a machete hidden in her áo dài."

Curtis didn't doubt the story. But he also knew how too many Americans had used the men and women of this country for their own ends, some knowing full well that was the case, others naively believing they were doing good.

He'd played a small role himself, he believed, as an Army journalist. Still, he'd added his abilities to a process that failed at a high cost to others. Curtis was an old soldier, too. And like everyone else at this reunion, he was struggling to come to terms with past, present, and future.

Chapter Six: Steps

At the end of the afternoon session Janet and her friend Betty Donaldson agreed to meet Curtis for dinner at the Midwest Mother Road Motel. Before then he had time to take his nostalgic hike in the woods.

Curtis and his childhood friends had generally entered the woods from the east, going down a gravel lane between two houses. At the end of a one-hundred-yard curving driveway off Limestone was the Estes' house, sitting at the crest of a small hill and looking down on a pond.

When he gave Beth a quick call to explain his plans, she asked, after a significant pause, "But you will have someone go with you?"

He laughed. "Not to worry. There aren't any meth labs guarded by pit bulls and degenerate hillbillies in these woods . . . at least I don't think there are."

Following the driveway down a slope until it curved south and rose toward the house, Circle boys and girls slipped off to the right, where a path went around the pond's northern edge. The railroad tracks ran to their right on a high embankment. Past the pond, the woods spread out to the west, widening like a fan between the tracks which angled northwest and a ridge to the south. The pond would be the central landmark of his current journey from west to east.

From the motel, he would retrace the steps of his boyhood self back to the pond, up the driveway, into the Circle, and past the house he'd grown up in. He was starting at the wide end of the fan in the woods and would come out at its narrowest point, the Estes' driveway. From there he would return to The Midwest Mother Road Motel via streets and sidewalks.

The posted warning signs Curtis encountered seemed to him generic and inconsequential: "no Trespassing" on railroad property; "Keep Out" of the enclosed mine area; "No Hunting" along barbed wire fences (most in need of repair). He would simply follow the creek that ran in the center of the fan back to where it issued from the west bank of the Estes' pond. Still, as he circumnavigated the forbidden areas, he knew he should be careful not to become disoriented.

When he heard a train coming toward him from town, he scrambled a bit awkwardly away from the 20-foot-high embankment. On a long downhill stretch, the train would be moving rapidly after the last crossroad, and he felt it wise to be invisible to officials.

He did ask himself if was reasonable for a man his age to be crouching behind a rocky outcrop—as he had when a boy—to avoid being spotted. He chuckled. But he was made uneasy by some specific memory of hiking this same path. He pushed it back down into his subconscious.

Moving east as the rest of the train passed above on his left, he encountered bushes, small trees (mostly scrub oak and cedar), creek branches, rocky patches, and tangled brush that did not provide landmarks. At times he veered south or north of the water's course.

The path—created, he assumed, by woodland critters—was not always distinct in grass or over rocks. When it appeared to cross the creek bed, its resumption on the other side was sometimes difficult to spot.

At one point he paused and found he had no cellular reception. That didn't stop him from imagining his wife's voice: "Really? You're in the woods alone an hour before dark, in a place that could have changed quite a bit since you hiked there fifty years ago?"

He imagined responding. "I could see from the railroad embankment It's all woods like it was. No campfire smoke from tramps following the rails; no wild sounds of witches gathering to induct innocent children into Satan's church; no sorority sisters seducing innocent high school boys into initiation rites so bacchanalian that their cries of joy rise up over the trees."

His phantom conversation dwindled when he heard a ringing from the railroad up on the embankment. There was no accompanying roar of a locomotive, though, and no whistles. Uh-oh, it could be one those little repair cars the company sends out to inspect potential trouble spots on the rails . . . or to catch trespassers up to no good along the right of way.

For a second time, he looked for something to duck behind (in this case, a mound of dirt) where Beth's voice sounded in his head a second time. "Fine. Now you're going to be arrested by the railroad and hauled in to appear before a judge for . . . " She couldn't think of a suitable crime. "For taking pictures for a rival railroad."

"I don't think the mechanics of railroad tracks are trade secrets," he answered. "And if they are, my phone has only pictures of Hillbilly Shed."

Still hiding, Curtis recalled a favorite scene from *O, Brother, Where art Thou?* The four escaped convicts, running from troopers and hounds, hear a man pumping a hand car down a railroad track. He's blind, but a seer like Teiresias in the movie's inspiration, Homer's *The Odyssey*. The sage, who has been both man and woman, tells them they "must travel a long, difficult road."

No hand car appeared, but another sound broke into Curtis' fantasy, a small engine somewhere behind him, probably up that little valley to the south. It sounded like a riding lawn mower, though that made no sense out here. Illogically, he imagined a young Katheryn Fahr, played by Holly Hunter, from *O, Brother*, pursuing him for . . . for something he couldn't even tell Beth he imagined. Then he had another worry: moonshiners or degenerate drug lords.

Recently he'd watched a movie about meth makers in a Missouri subculture, inbred clans living on worn out farmland. The characters were Ozark mountain families stereotyped in many Hollywood shows like *The Beverly Hillbillies*; but there was no humor in this film.

Bone Hearts featured a thirteen-year-old girl whose father is murdered by a rival clan, and she represents the only— probably the last—trace of decency in a decadent community. The novel and the movie made her people look as bad as the warring tribes along the Afghanistan-Pakistan border region—at least as pictured by American media.

Curtis had hated the movie, not that it didn't present a believable portrait of debased human culture. But its considerable box office and critical success endorsed a view of his home state that was grotesque. And the screenwriter (also the novel's author) was a Missourian.

From behind a tree Curtis saw an all-terrain four-wheeler coming along the side of the ridge south of the creek. An overweight man in camouflage and a backward facing baseball hat gripped the handlebars. He was not swinging around turns and pulling the handlebars up to do a wheelie, joy riding. Instead, he cruised, sometimes looking up into woods on his right and then down toward the creek on his left.

"He's a homegrown, gun-toting terrorist," whispered his fictional Beth in his ear. "You're about to stumble onto one of his stills. Or discover his daughter, Betty Lou, swimming nude in the creek!"

"Nonsense," he imagined whispering back. "He's just taking a recreational spin around the neighborhood." But Curtis knew of no neighborhood in the direction the rider came from, and he'd seen no signs of one from his original vantage point on Mine Road.

"To think 45 five years of our marriage will end with the crack of a crowbar so close to your childhood home. Go down fighting, my love."

After the rider returned the way he had come, Curtis hurried ahead and came to the pond; but he was south instead of north of it, as it was on his left not his right. He didn't want to cross the Estes' (or current owner's) yard to get to the driveway, though he couldn't actually see the house through the trees. So, he continued southeast.

In his teenage years, the town had put a small park in that area, and he soon found the chain link fence on its western edge. But it was eight feet tall with no gate.

Okay, up and over, he thought putting the toe of one shoe in the fence and lacing the fingers of his hands into the mesh at shoulder height. He'd done this many a time. He pulled up with his hands, lifting his other foot to press into the fence eighteen inches above the first. Hanging there perhaps ten seconds, he slid down to the ground. He was not going to climb this fence.

How far around the park would this fence go? And which way should he go? Was he on the south or the north side of the pond? Now that he asked himself, was this even Estes Pond? Where the hell, in fact, was he?

Chapter Seven: Review

Then his phone rang.

"Are you back at the motel?" The voice of his real wife was a bit testy where his fantasy one had been teasing.

"Almost. Just, um, leaving the woods to walk back via old Route 66. Twenty minutes. Everything okay with you?"

He hoped to switch the topic from him to her, though it was not likely anything had changed in North Carolina over the last hour and a half.

"I'm good. Of course, your dogs miss you."

They had two cocker spaniels, sisters from the same litter. And he was generally the one who fed them.

"I take it from this call that you, too, miss me."

"Humph. Call when you're back at the motel."

Curtis hung up and realized he must now have a signal. He switched to his GPS, which he hoped would give him his location. It did, and he saw that he was only a few hundred yards west of Ridgewood Drive, the extension of Limestone south from the Circle. All he had to do was get around this fenced-in park and he would be back in familiar territory.

Prompted by a vague memory, he moved south. Wasn't there a place where rainwater had dug a gap under the fence, small enough for a 15-year-old to slip beneath? Of course, the older version of that boy was taller, heavier, and far less agile. But he'd survived potential embarrassment by hiding in the woods several times already. He would now have to lower himself—literally—to crawl on hands and knees and escape the woods that captured the elderly.

Fifteen minutes later, he was upright and striding past the house he'd grown up in, a self-satisfied smile on his face. Ha! Hike in the woods Déjà Vu.

He was not likely to tell his dinner companions at the Mother Road about his trek, however. They would see him as the eccentric, lonely kid he'd been fifty years ago. But he did imagine himself back home entertaining a small social gathering with a Show Me tale "inspired by real events." If he had wanted to narrate his late afternoon recreation today, though, the story his classmate Betty shared would have shown him how trivial it would be.

Their conversation over the house special of lasagna (his vegetarian) plus the salad bar was enjoyable—all about kids, grandkids, travel, retirement hopes, a few of the inevitable health problems. When he slipped in a plea for help selling the scholarship idea, he unleashed a flood of resentment.

"I don't get it," Betty exclaimed. "Kids these days expect us to bail them out of their mistakes and pony up for four—or six!—years of partying at college. When we were their age," she pointed a fork at Janet, "we had to own up, didn't we, to our mistakes and earn the money to go to school."

Curtis tried not to show surprise.

Turning the fork toward him, Betty went on. "And I'll tell you this, Professor, girls back then had more obstacles to overcome than you boys, but nobody stepped up to give us a free ride."

Janet nodded agreement at her but glanced at Curtis also, as if to say, "I told you so." He realized he didn't know either of their personal histories well and had assumed they'd been able to take advantage of the same opportunities he had.

"Janet chose one of the few fields women could study in at the time, art," continued Betty. "And, of course, that actually meant art education. Teaching, nursing, home economics—they were our focus on the way to what really mattered, the M.R.S. degree."

Curtis thought of his sister who turned down scholarships to enlist in the Army. Had she decided she was going to be channeled into math education or blocked from emerging technical fields? He'd never considered her decision as much beyond rebellion—at least, at first.

Janet touched Betty's hand. "And, sadly, when we fulfilled our destiny as wives and homemakers, our men's eyes and hands wandered. Somehow that was okay for them, but a surefire path to divorce for us."

"Well, yes," Curtis agreed. "I didn't mean to suggest many girls—women—weren't hemmed in by the system. My wife, for instance . . ."

Betty interrupted him. "Listen, I'm glad she and her family are in a position to help others by endowing a scholarship, but . . ."

She signaled for another glass of wine. Janet took out the menu to consider desserts.

"And, you know," Betty went on, "this kind of irritates me: Patrick's letter implies we're all reasonably comfortable, not having to work in our retirement. When my first husband's alimony ended, I had to go back to work as a secretary—low pay, no retirement, no healthcare. I still put in twenty to thirty hours a week to earn enough for a little travel or to buy a new car."

"Oh, I'm sorry. I didn't know you were divorced. I thought . . ."

"Oh, I have a husband, a pretty good one. He's ten years older. That helps."

The wine came, and Janet ordered a piece of apple pie. Curtis felt it would be appropriate to order one, too. But he thought about what Betty said and about Patrick's confidence his classmates were "comfortable." Patrick had been an excellent student, a three-sport athlete, an attractive, desirable date.

Betty leaned back in her chair and studied him. "Did you ever look at me in high school?" The question seemed to him to come out of nowhere. "I mean, actually look at me."

"Well, of course. I mean I saw students. I knew who you were, though I guess I wasn't quite in your group."

"The last months of our senior year? That spring?"

Okay, he thought. I'm about to be accused of being some

sort of ogler. And it was true that, given the restrictive social code, a lot of boys lusted from afar. As his wife had taught him, the girls knew what the bizarre looks on their faces meant.

There were the lucky guys, of course—the jocks, who, if their boasting was true, enjoyed the favors of many girls. But he didn't fit in that category.

Being admired for intelligence—"brains," they were called—seemed to him at least to make the day- and night-dreams of petting even more distant (literally). It was as if such physical activities would be beneath those in the running for valedictorian.

Was Betty in one of his classes that year? He couldn't re-member. He did know where she lived because it was a nice house and on one of the regular ways he walked to and from home and school. Then again, in such a small town with fa-miliar neighborhoods, he knew where most of the girls he would have liked to date lived.

Fairfield was informally divided by Main Street into an east and a west side. There had been, for example, an East Elementary, where she had attended, and a West Elementary, where he and Janet went to school. Fairfield High School, which brought everyone together, was in the east half. Still, even in elementary school the boys rode their bikes all over town, and by ninth grade students from east and west merged into one body.

While the term "stalker" was not used in those days, it might apply to many awkward teenage boys on apparently aimless walks hoping to run into teenage girls. They'd tell their parents they'd gone out to "visit a friend, to get something downtown, to look for the pocketknife that had inexplicably slipped from their pants. But the only one who might legitimately accuse him of that would have been Kathryn Fahr.

Janet now joined Betty in grilling Curtis. "What did she wear those last months? Most of us wore skirts and blouses tucked in at the waist."

He did remember that slacks were not allowed. "Listen," he admitted," I'm sure Carol and our mother discussed the clothes she should wear, but I guarantee you I paid no attention. I assume the two of you dressed pretty much alike."

"No," Betty said, "At least not in the final weeks of the term. If I said the final 'trimester,' would that mean anything to you?"

And then Curtis understood: she'd been pregnant. If the school had found out, she would have been expelled. And finishing later, as a mother, would have been difficult. "Ah, so you dressed to hide a pregnancy. I had no idea."

"Eugene and I were secretly married in early May, but the families didn't announce the fact until into the summer. By then we'd moved to Columbia, ostensibly for him to start at the university in the fall. But in a few months I went to 'visit' an aunt in Illinois and came back with a baby girl. She's the only good thing that came out of my senior year."

She tossed back the last of her wine. Curtis winced.

Chapter Eight: Emblems

When Curtis checked out of the Midwest Mother Road in the morning, he was surprised to find that a message had been taken for him at the desk. "Jackson Castle," it read, "says if Mr. Lindbloom still wants to find his h.s. friend, he should stop by Mr. Castle's house before leaving town." Since he wasn't due back at his brother's until evening, he could go after lunch. It might be a time to raise the idea of renting the Castles' old house.

Understanding now some of the reasons for resistance to a scholarship drive, Curtis decided not to bring up the issue during breakfast at Fanny's Dairy Delite, the last get together of the weekend. Back in Cypress, he would consult with Patrick by phone on next steps.

Because of his research into women who worked at or ran motels, restaurants, and gift shops along Route 66, he was eager to study the current Dairy Delite. It had been owned and operated by women years ago and thus was a potential subject for his planned book, "Roadside Attractions along America's Main Street."

Beth had questioned his proposed title on feminist grounds: women were not objects. He claimed this was just tentative and referred to establishments, not people. But he kept to himself the belief that, in America, sex sells books like everything else. He imagined a number of suggestive cover designs, not the least of which was some version of the Dairy Delite's "Fanny."

The marketing of female representation came up in discussion when someone asked Barbara Lemon if it was true Rebecca Bright, a class beauty, was not coming to the reunion.

"Well, she says her schedule is pretty tight, but, if you ask me, that's stretching it for our event that's more than a year off."

"She does move in busy circles," admitted Jim, the mayor.

"She mentioned no particular engagements, health problems, or travel difficulties," noted John Robinson. "Wouldn't so famous a person want to inspect the very ordinary place from which she'd risen so high?" After college, Rebecca had been signed to a movie contract and starred in a television how, *Planet of the Titans*.

She'd been popular in high school—cheerleader, a star in every dramatic performance, one of the princesses in the homecoming court. Her achievements earned her a scholarship to a school of performing arts in Kansas City. From there she went to Hollywood.

Barbara explained, "She's lived out West so long, I don't know the last time she came back. Some of us move on, you know."

Some, like Barbara, thought Curtis, stayed put. That was another division of the class that developed over time and would be revealed in the yearbook address list.

Betty offered. "Someone told me she learned the hard way about how to succeed in show business—if you're a woman, that is."

Tim Carlson objected. "Good looks are necessary for men as well as women. And the men don't have anything . . . anything extra to offer with them."

"We don't offer!" said Betty with some anger. "Men take."

Janet clucked he tongue. "Some men also offer."

Carol Yates held up a hand. "Whoa! Let's not turn this into an argument. We're here to plan a party, not pick sides."

They all nodded, though Betty kept quiet for a time. Curtis raised the question about meal choices for the two major events: heavy hors d'oeuvres for the cocktail hour on Friday night, banquet on Saturday. He didn't say he was vegetarian (though, because he ate fish, he was more technically a pescatarian), but he hoped someone would. And it turned out the mayor had a favorite caterer who handled a lot of town contracts and was therefore familiar with dietary needs, especially for seniors: gluten free, vegan, low sugar.

As that discussion went on—fortunately in a pleasant tone—Curtis thought about men as sex objects. Not to women but to other men. There had been no openly gay boys in high school, only rumors about those who "played the piano" or "didn't date" or were "mama's boys".

In college environments, homosexuality might have been more openly talked about but not accepted the way it would be in later generations. Reviewing the original *Confluence* back in North Carolina, Curtis had paused at the picture of Sammy Benton, an intelligent, handsome, kind boy. What had become of him?

Curtis often ended up walking to or from school with him. Smart and skilled in drawing, he talked about becoming an architect. He was the youngest of six children and the only boy of parents who ran a neighborhood grocery store in between the Circle and downtown.

Although he had to work at Benton's Store like his siblings, he spent more time, it seemed to Curtis, arranging fruit and vegetable displays than hauling produce. He refused to work with the butcher. He was more interested in the clothes he wore and how he had his hair cut than Curtis was. Some guys called him a "sissy," which didn't necessarily mean they thought he was gay. But they would sometimes raise an arm and drop the hand in what they understood as a feminine gesture. Whether he was or was not homosexual, these acts were cruel.

Were some girls attracted to other girls? There had been few exclusively female associations—no sports teams, unless you counted cheerleading. Curtis didn't remember seeing any all-female groups except the homecoming court pictured in the original yearbook.

Conventional wisdom held that the talk at slumber parties was mostly about boys, with some discussion of boys and girls outside the group who were liked or disliked. But were "pillow fights," wondered Curtis, a metaphor?

He looked around Fanny's Dairy Delite. The present building was a replica, but a succinct institutional history of the 1952 original was pictured on the back of their menu. Mrs. Flora Hamilton, retired nurse, and her friend Madeline Powers, former elementary school teacher, started the business in a nondescript metal shed with a rounded roof. The founders were entrepreneurs who recognized that people would be traveling more in the post-war boom. Returning soldiers brought a renewed confidence to the country and inspired journeys to other places and holiday travel down the Mother Road.

Originally the drive-in ice cream store had been on Route 66, but, when the first by-pass, a three-lane highway, was built around town, the owners of Fanny's had to invest in billboards on the approaches to Fairfield. Thanks to their advertising and the town's growth, they had regular traffic most of the year and did a heavy business throughout the summer months.

For their publicity campaign the two women created a

distinctive emblem: the outline of a motherly figure, "Fanny." The slightly stout, cheerful matron sporting an apron and waving a welcome appeared on dozens of billboards along Route 66 to the east and west.

As the meeting was breaking up, Curtis had a chance to ask the mayor about the current establishment. "I hope the proprietor is a descendent of the original founders," he said.

Jimmy laughed. "Not at all. A group of businessmen in Tulsa have been buying up places close to university campuses all along the interstate. Students these days carry around their parents' credit cards and don't hesitate at $3.00 coffee and $7.00 ice cream treats."

"Hmm. I did think the prices a bit high, especially compared to when you could get five cent and ten cent cones. So, did they pay for the logo and design features?"

The sugar and napkin containers had the Route 66 highway sign on the sides, and the placemats featured a Missouri map with the original highway highlighted. Curtis looked around at the booths, the ice cream and soda machines behind the counter, the old photos on the walls.

"A lot of this is in the public domain," explained Jim. "But a proposal did come through town council, which reviews applications for licenses and permits. Most of the members are more interested in expanding trade than preserving landmarks. As I remember, the group claimed that descendants of the founders raised no objection to use of old material."

"I came here a lot, on weekends mostly, but sometimes after school, too. You know, I don't remember having a lot of time to waste. Most of us had jobs after school and chores at home on weekends."

Jim agreed, "Now everywhere has wi-fi; they bring their

laptops. As long as there's space, they can sit here all after-noon."

"Things aren't the way they were," laughed Curtis. "And sometimes I think they never were."

In fact, he was beginning to question the idea of "Déjà Vu" itself, returning to a view of the world that had shaped his youth but that might not be adequate for the present, let alone the future.

When he reached his car in the parking lot, Curtis looked up at the sign above the front door. This Fanny was signifi-cantly less matronly than the original. And the youthful phys-ical specimen smiling over her shoulder reshaped—literal-ly—the meaning of her name.

Chapter Nine: Places

Just as Curtis was preparing to back out of his parking place, Janet, with Betty in the passenger seat, pulled her car into the space beside him and signaling him to roll down his window.

"Listen," Betty said across the space between the two cars. "I'm sorry I unloaded last night. It just boiled over, but I didn't need to pin my frustration on you."

"No problem. A lot of emotions we've bottled up over the years are breaking into the open. Gary got into a long tale from Vietnam that clearly haunts him."

"Okay, thanks. So, one other thing. I know you're trying to find Bill Castle. Anyone else you especially want to contact?"

"Now that you ask, can you tell me anything about Cindy Martin?"

"Susan Howe, too?"

"Why, yes. How did you guess?"

She gestured to Janet to turn the car off. Curtis decided he might as well also. This was reminding him of the iconic high school rendezvous at a drive-in restaurant—hm, maybe Déjà Vu, after all.

"If you remember," Betty resumed, "I worked as a sales-clerk at Castle Clothes, which was run by Bill's mom. She talked about your weekend bridge parties. Are you hoping to get the old gang back together again?"

Mrs. Castle was a widow by the time the boys were coming over to play cards. And Jackson had moved out, so she enjoyed having company.

"As a matter of fact, yes, something like that. Mrs. Castle taught us the basics of bridge, while providing ample snacks and drinks. A nice lady."

"She was good to me, too. I'll tell you about that another time. But she enjoyed you guys. She suggested you were not dating a lot, so it was good you had . . . a social life of your own."

Curtis winced. "Well, we did go on dates . . . now and then. But you're right that we saw those nights as escape from the pressures at school!"

"Ha," interjected Janet from the other side of Betty. "The only pressures you faced were who would be valedictorian and who would get the best scholarship offers."

Curtis ignored her and said to Betty, "So, the other two

card sharks, what do you know that might help me recruit them . . . for the reunion."

"Okay, I can tell you this: Cindy's going to be a hard sell. Lives in Springfield, IL. I'll see if I have an address back home and email you."

"A hard sell,?" wondered Curtis. What did that mean? "And Susan Howe?"

"I know she's a ridiculously busy woman, still practicing medicine and on all sorts of boards and charities. She may even have her own Foundation, something to do with women's health. Barbara's got her phone number. A call from you would be better than email."

He nodded. She leaned back into her seat, rolled the window up, and waved good-bye.

Seeing others from the group coming out of Fanny's Dairy Delite, he remembered how both planned and chance encounters had occurred here on a regular basis throughout their teenage years. Now the phenomenon had resumed, at least for this weekend.

Because Curtis had never moved easily in this environment, he had generally been outside the exciting interactions of his classmates. He might come in, stand in line, make a purchase, say hi to a few he recognized. But he would leave shortly, observing others in animated conversation, his only real gain the eating of the ice cream.

Now, as he pulled onto Kingshighway, recently also labeled "Historic Route 66," the pattern of the past led him to imagine some of his female classmates still at Fanny's—jumping into each other backseats to share tales about children and grandchildren while the men leaned on car fenders and talked about college and professional football. Here he was, headed toward town, out of the center of it all once again. Still, he'd had good conversations with Gary, Janet, and Betty. And in the spring he would concentrate on making more connections.

The new Castle house was in one of the fancy developments close to the country club. He knew that similar developments had grown up over the last twenty years, but he'd never explored them. When he was here, he'd spent his time with his parents, who had moved from a small, older home in an established neighborhood to a new development across town.

The residential subdivisions he drove past now featured McMansions, two- and three-story homes with multi-car garages, swimming pools, gazebos and fountains. He saw no children playing, no bicycles parked or moving, no dogs running loose—standard features of the Circle in the past. Fairfield had prospered like much of America, but people lived indoors more, traveled by car not foot, manicured their property to present almost a model of contemporary life rather than its reality. He was glad his walk in the woods had allowed him to see the skeleton of the town he'd grown up in—distinct, modest neighborhoods with active families.

He knew the original campus building where his father had taught was at the heart of an expanded campus. And the string of shops downtown, like the Table, still existed, though they catered to university students while locals shopped at Walmart and surrounding chain business.

A few miles out of town, he turned onto a road with divided lanes winding across a field and into a stand of woods. He followed Elm Thoroughfare to a stone gateway with a speaker set in a brick column. Walls stretched left and right with a sign identifying this neighborhood as "Forest Estates."

On the column the words, "Enter code or press #," were printed beside the speaker. Pressing #, he announced to an unseen guard who he was and that he was here to visit Jackson Castle. Perhaps he should have said "the Castles' house," to make it clear he knew it wasn't an actual castle. "Please wait," said a woman's voice.

Shortly, he was told to advance to a second gate. There he showed "a picture ID, please" which the guard, wearing a private security firm uniform, scanned. Walking to the back of the car, she took a picture of the license, handed a "Visitor" sign for him to put on his dash, and gave him a map with the route to 18 Cedar Way. He was to return the sign on checking out. He saw it was time stamped.

Jackson, whose house did resemble a castle, a very quiet one, met him at the door and led him into a study off the main hall. Again, he gestured for Curtis to sit as he straightened some papers on his desk, which was as large and fine as the one at the bank.

"I've spoken with my brother Bill, and, somewhat to my surprise, he said he'd like to see you. He lives on a somewhat remote place in southwestern Phipps County, about a twenty-minute drive from here." He pushed a sheet of paper across the desk.

Curtis looked over the map. "I take it he doesn't get out much?"

"That's correct. He's a recluse by choice. We . . . the family . . . let him move out to this old farm . . . let's see . . . more than thirty years ago. The 60's you know; he just dropped out."

"Would it be okay to try today? If he has a phone, I could call ahead."

Since Curtis didn't fly out of St. Louis until tomorrow, he

should have time to visit and still get to Louis' by evening.

Jackson shook his head. "No phone. But, given what I've told him about you and your classmates meeting this week-end, he's aware of the possibility. Now, I see you're driving a Jeep Wrangler, good. That should get there. The . . . um . . . last few miles are a bit rugged."

"Okay. I guess I'll give this a go, since I probably won't be back this way until next spring." He rose but then added. "Oh, one other thing.

Jackson raised his eyebrows.

Curtis went on. "The reunion committee is looking at dates and housing options. When that's settled, I will have a per-sonal request. It may seem a bit odd, but is there any chance you would consider renting the old family home to a few of us? We'd pay your renters for just a couple of evenings. We'd bring our own refreshments, not spend the night, just have a quiet party. Sort of a return to an old place for a small group that, um, would include Bill."

Jackson studied him. "I suppose it's possible. When you've selected a date, let me know. Maybe that would draw Bill out of his hermitage."

"Yes, that would be an added incentive. I appreciate it."

He reached over to shake hands. Jackson held his a bit lon-ger than expected. Looking down at his desk, he said, "When you see Bill's house—it's pretty deep in the woods, so it'll be right in front of you all of a sudden, it would be a good idea to have a white handkerchief or towel to wave out of the win-dow. You know, kind of a signal."

"A signal?" wondered Curtis. A signal what . . . not to shoot?

Chapter Ten: Flags

Heading south, Curtis realized he wanted to talk to his mom about Fairfield families. Teenagers obviously talked about each other. And he assumed that parents discussed with their friends the behavior of their children. But it hadn't ever occurred to him that parents might also share reports about some teenagers with other teenagers, as Mrs. Castle must have done with Betty, giving her a picture of him from the perspective of his elders. Had there been a version of him that was shared by his friends' parents but which was never known to him?

As he cruised past Fairfield's city limits, the map from Jackson beside him on the car seat, he glanced at familiar landmarks. He had about fifteen miles to go on this road, recently improved by the removal of sharp turns, before he would take a small state road west. Then there were several county roads to follow, probably gravel and in places difficult to navigate.

If the older generation did talk regularly about the younger one, they would build a portrait of their offspring's activity somewhat removed from the facts. Given the usual weakness--amplifying in public their children's accomplishments and minimizing their shortcomings--it was likely that any version Betty heard about what happened on Friday nights in Fairfield was several removes from actuality.

He recalled being told to draw a cat in elementary school. Try as he could to reproduce the simple outline of ears, head, body, tail on the notepad at his desk, his cat was always bloated somewhere, shrunken in other places. Even when he took the model drawing home and tried to trace it on a thin piece of paper, his fat wayward pencil inevitably strayed to form its own creature. Adults' picture of him as a child was possibly similarly distorted.

He drove past the old swimming pool on one side of the U.S. highway south. Everyone referred to it as a "pool," but it was really a natural rock basin in a spring-fed stream. An enterprising family had augmented the area around it with picnic tables sporting umbrellas, unpainted wooden dressing booths, and a concession stand. The water was unfiltered and flowed continuously, if slowly, across the basin and down-stream through a low concrete dam.

No one questioned the conditions there until the town build a municipal pool where lifeguards were on duty, chlorine pu-rified the water, and low and high diving boards providing ex-citing activity. Cool Pool survived only a few years after that.

Curtis liked how the old pool had been integrated with the landscape. Like so many elements of the modern city, the town pool was positioned in terms of accessibility, not geog-raphy. The more users, the more profitable the operation, so it was built near the schools and the center of Fairfield. Town water came from wells miles away, pumped to a high tower on the north side of town. Gravity then delivered it to homes, businesses, and the town pool.

The woods of his childhood would also eventually lose their shape to new roads, parks, storm drainage ditches, cul-verts, and sewer pipes. His generation might tell their grand-children what it used to be like, but the reality before the young's eyes would blot out remembered feature es like the low and the high trail, the creeks and the paths lost in a new landscape.

If the term " Déjà Vu" meant for Curtis the restoration of structures that shaped and sustained his generation's child-hood, the project was probably doomed. But if the collective memories of reunion participants could bring before them a past informed by the perspective of age, they might recover who they'd been and see the path that guided them to where they were. What enduring principles would be discovered?

He turned west on a blacktop state road that climbed up the side of a long east-west ridge, pushed along by glaciers eons ago. He followed it for several miles, took a gravel road, perhaps originally an access road for lumber companies, down into a valley. It came to a dead end after three quarters of a mile at the edge of a clearing, a primitive cabin at its center. Curtis dangled a white handkerchief out the car window.

He didn't recognize the man who stepped out on the porch as an older version of his high school friend. This figure was lean where Bill had been stocky, hunched when Bill had stood straight, grim-faced rather than alert and ready to make a joke, grizzled and gray as opposed to fair-haired, clean shaven, well dressed. Still, this stranger waved Curtis toward him.

"Your brother told you I'd be coming, I take it?" Curtis offered.

"He did." He looked past Curtis and his car, as if he suspected there were others in the area. "Long time."

Curtis laughed, "Damn near 50 years. A reason for my appearance."

"Come in, then," Bill said and preceded him into the cabin.

There was a single room with a kitchen area at one end, a ladder nailed to the wall for access to a loft, and a door to what Curtis assumed was a bathroom in the back. (An outhouse, though, would not have surprised him.) There was a table with two chairs by the stove and a sofa, perhaps a sofa bed, in the middle of the room. Three cane bottomed chairs stacked with books and magazines were scattered about; articles of clothing hung from the backs.

"Cozy. You . . . live here now?"

"It's quiet." He made no gesture to offer Curtis a drink or act the host in any way.

"I see. Yes." He gestured toward a chair at the table. "May I?"

"Help yourself." Bill remained standing at the end of the sofa.

Curtis turned the chair toward him and sat down. "Well, did Jackson tell you our class is planning a reunion next fall? I kind of fell into putting together a booklet about where we all are, what we're doing, that sort of thing. And no one seemed to be able to say exactly where you are."

"Huh!"

"And, you know, we saw a lot of each other those last years of school, so I wanted to make a special effort to . . . to get in touch."

"Well, you've done it."

Curtis scanned the room another time: no television, computer, telephone. Few books but more than a dozen wooden boxes that appeared to be full of papers. By the door was a gun cabinet with what he guessed were shotguns and one deer rifle.

"So, a reunion doesn't interest you. A lot skip earlier ones—10, 20 years; but this is big."

Bill's smile was crooked, but he did seem to be amused. "Oh, I didn't say that exactly. It's unlikely I'll come—I don't get out much." He chuckled. "But I might appreciate knowing what's going to happen, the when and the where."

"Oh, I can give you regular updates, keep you in the loop. Do you get mail here?"

Another chuckle. "Jackson will get it to me. He and I, we're all that's left of the once grand Castle family. And I think he kind of worries about me. Maybe he should."

"You ever married, had children?"

"Castles aren't easy to live with."

"I see. Well, I guess I'd better get on back then. I'll spend the night with my brother in St. Louis, fly home to North Carolina tomorrow."

This elicited no questions about his family, his history. But Bill's face suddenly lit up.

"Hey, you remember this?" He pulled a rolled sheet of paper out from behind his sofa and brought it over to the table. Curtis had to turn his chair around to see what he was doing.

"This goes way back," Bill said with some pleasure and unrolled the map of the town's sewer system, his science fair project from half a century earlier.

Now Curtis chuckled. "I do. Carol, my sister, was reminding me of it . . . recently."

Again, Bill asked no questions. "This was the piece de resistance of my high school—the final process of Fairfield's life support system. You know, like the vessels that take blood from all parts of the body through the kidneys to be filtered. This flushes out all the waste from town."

Curtis studied it. Then he noticed that some of the marks on the yellowed paper appeared to be new, notations in blue whereas the original, he was pretty sure, had been all in black. There were several paths of arrows from the city limits into the center.

"You . . . you, um, still work on this?"

"Oh, now and then, just for my amusement, you see. I get Jackson to give me updates on how the town grows, where . . . um, new developments go in, changes in landscape." He gestured at areas that hadn't been built up when they lived there.

"Very nice." Curtis was going to say the reunion event would be a similar effort to update everyone's understanding when he noticed a small red X at the courthouse.

"Say," Bill said, suddenly rolling up his map. "Let me know the time and the place of the reunion when it's fixed, okay? I probably won't come, but it might be nice to know."

Curtis wanted to ask exactly why he wanted to know but resisted the impulse. The answer might require the cancellation of Bridge Game Déjà Vu. . . and more.

Book Two: Cindy
Chapter Eleven: Cave

Over the winter, Curtis secured a second, though conditional, commitment to Bridge Game Déjà Vu. Cindy Martin agreed to come—providing Curtis could find certain town records for her that she'd been unable to obtain long-distance. Whatever had alienated Cindy from the town some years ago, Curtis concluded, might become a reason to return, although to what end he couldn't tell. He promised to see what he could do.

Her unspoken intentions added to Curtis' growing sense that we often entertain incorrect portraits of our fellow travelers. His wife, for instance, could not comprehend what lay behind some of his classmate's thinking to resist the scholarship idea. Her mother-in-law helped clarify.

Curtis' mother Mirian/Mid had sold the home she and Oscar had owned in Fairfield when her husband Oscar passed away; and she was comfortably settled in a retirement home outside of Harbor City.

At one of her usual Sunday dinners in her son's home early in later in the year Mid tried to explain Midwestern views to Beth. "A first principle," she said, "is 'Take care of yourself. It derives from the philosophy of pioneers coming west: if you had to be helped along the way, you weren't strong enough to survive life on the frontier."

Curtis added, "It's part of the New England ethos also, Emerson's self-reliance. He valued independence, the ability to trust yourself more than institutional authority. And those are not qualities to dismiss, even if some misuse them for selfish ends."

Beth said, "I lean toward the idea that 'it takes a village to raise a child,' especially as few of us are leading a frontier life today." She shook her head. "But I have learned that some people have to believe they ask nothing of society."

"Well, thinking about that, Patrick and I are considering other ways to argue for the fund at the spring meeting. But Mom, your reference to communal values reminds me: did parents in Fairfield regularly discuss their children and their peers when we were growing up, measuring us against social standards of the time . . . well, and against each other?"

She chuckled, "Sure, now and then we traded what we knew of your doings, but not necessarily in order to judge you. I'm sure you and Beth wanted to know how your three— Justin, Carl, and Mary Anne—fit in their school groups."

"Yeah, I guess so. But after the fact, we've learned that we didn't always see things accurately." Curtis was sensitive to this idea of judgment by peers because his return to Fairfield had him toggling between the states of an insecure youngster and confident senior. Both selves, of course, were potentially misunderstood. And, he had to admit, if adults form pictures of their children that are not always accurate, so, too, do kids mischaracterize the older generation.

"I guess I can understand parents talking to other parents," Curtis admitted, "but did some parents share inside family information with kids from other homes?"

"Well, your father and I seldom saw any of your friends when they weren't with you."

Curtis said. "Okay. Being church goers and a bit more civic minded, though, Beth and I attended a lot of social occasions where we interacted with our children's friends."

Beth nodded. "We tended to steer clear of gossip, though."

His mother asked, "Hmm. Are there some specific cases of parents sharing information you've turned up in getting biographical sketches from classmates?"

"No, not really. I did find out that Cindy Martin has some sort of disagreement or misunderstanding with someone or some people in Fairfield ten, fifteen years ago. She's a bit of hard sell in terms of coming to the reunion."

Even after his years in college and graduate school, he thought of Mrs. Martin as one of the best teachers he'd ever had. She'd insisted that her students watch NBC's *The Huntley Brinkley Report* every night. Before that, Curtis had little idea of the things going on the nation and beyond. The process of expanding the frame of reference within which he viewed the world became a habit, as she'd intended. It continued, in fact, to his spring visit to his old hometown where, once again, he found himself revising his version of the past and the present.

As he had in the fall, Curtis flew into St. Louis and spent a night with his brother Louis and wife Suzanne. However, instead of heading southwest down to Fairfield the next morning, he'd decided to tour Missouri's most famous cave, childhood hideout of Samuel Clemons/Mark Twain and his childhood friends. Inspired by a Huck Finn ready to light out for "The Territory," maybe Curtis would become more sympathetic to those who value self-sufficiency.

Boats run up to Hannibal and back daily from St. Louis. Other visitors drive down from Chicago or east from Kansas City, often feeling the trip as a pilgrimage to an American landmark. So, Curtis would listen to the crowd as well as to the tour guide.

Standing in line to purchase an entrance pass, he reflected that the adult he had become was influenced by the fictional characters—Tom Sawyer, Nattie Bumpo, D'Artagnan, John Carter of Mars—that had roamed his thoughts when he was a teenager. Would this tour reveal figures that had made him who he is and then disappeared into the shadows of his memory?

He had to admit to the college student who escorted him and a handful of other tourists into the labyrinth of tunnels, "Now, I am a little bit worried about tight spaces."

"There's a trick," said 'Tracy' (he read the name on her tag). "The passages are sometimes narrow in some places, but, if you look up, the ceilings are almost always way over your head. So, don't look at the walls; look up. That will give you a feeling of space."

Curtis had read that the cave, over six and a half miles in length, had over 250 passages. There was linear space, then, if not lateral, and, apparently, vertical space.

"Mark Twain Cave also has many rooms," added Tracy, "though they're not as large as those, say, in Onondaga or Meramec, James James' legendary hideout . . . and a place where Kate Smith famously sang 'God Bless America' in 1947"

"Ah, after the war," observed Curtis. "A time to be grateful for this country."

An elderly man in the group sighed, "Those days are gone, I'm afraid. We've lost our sense of patriotism, and now it's 'get what you can while you can.'" Curtis noticed the American flag pin on his shirt pocket.

"We pulled together after 9/11," added a woman who appeared to be taking two grandchildren on an outing. "But sadly, we get into these wars overseas, trying to help people who hate America. And now we're building a socialist state here at home where money is taken from those of us who work and given to those who don't."

Tracy must have recognized that this kind of talk would complicate the tour, so she launched into her narrative. "Thousands of people come here every year. They want to connect to American history, to our literary heroes."

"Not the young people," countered the man with the flag pin. "It's all about them."

Curtis knew that Twain, though one of the first distinctly American voices, spoke with a deep appreciation of ancient cultural traditions. In the 55-minute tour, they would pass places where Clemons the boy acted as if he were a character in the novels of the Scot Sir Walter Scott, Aladdin from the 1000-year-old Arabian Nights, and England's Robin Hood.

Although Huck Finn claims at the end of his narrative to be escaping the restraints of Becky Thatcher's civilization, he doesn't get away untouched. Neither would the present generation escape the fact they were citizens of the global community.

Curtis didn't realize yet how much his own trip back in time would force him to reevaluate the little world of his childhood. Revelations about how outside forces had shaped that community would explain, among other things, why Cindy Martin vowed never to come home.

"Now, if you'll come this way," said Tracy brightly, "we'll take a walk in one of the world's finest natural wonders." Wonderful, thought Curtis. Let us hope so.

In the conversation that followed, he was unhappy to witness an undercurrent of resentment that a black man was now president of these United States. Having lived in the South for over 40 years, he'd confronted firsthand the history of slavery and its legacy, both institutionalized and disguised racism.

With the group made up primarily of retirees, Curtis was not surprised at expressions reflecting a resistance to change, a desire to return to the good old days. He heard that sentiment a lot from his generation of educators—college isn't what it used to be.

Despite a few tremors of claustrophobia, Curtis generally enjoyed his walk into history. The "decline of America" discussion, though, caused him to worry—correctly, it would turn out—that similar sentiments would shape reunion discussion over the coming weekend.

Chapter Twelve: Rocks

After his tour, Curtis skirted the St. Louis suburbs and reached the interstate, which followed the path of the former Route 66. In his head he began to compose a possible editor's forward to the reunion yearbook. He might begin with an acknowledgement that his own success in life derived from the environment in which he—and, of course, his classmates—were raised. Yes, they worked hard, faced adversities, made sacrifices. But they were blessed from the beginning to grow up in a stable community with a commitment to the welfare of all.

He did have to make at least one major admission: the women in his class faced restrictions in their careers. Many of their mothers had worked in traditionally masculine jobs during the war, but then had been urged to leave them in peacetime. Most became hard-working stay-at-home housewives; but a significant percentage now wanted their daughters to have careers, perhaps in accepted roles as teachers or nurses, but also possibly in other professions.

The men had also faced challenges, being the last generation confronted with a military draft. Many served and returned to paths they had planned before service, taking on the role of breadwinner. But some did not come home; and the scars of the Vietnam War marked those who participated as well as those who opposed the unpopular conflict. Curtis knew a deep resentment festered among many veterans.

In *Confluence II* he would note that other communities in this country had not had the advantages Fairfield had provided its children. The Massive Resistance to integration in the 50's and 60's had fractured the South's social fabric, especially in the little college town where he and Beth had raised their children. While a private academy gave white children an education, schooling for most black children ended. They were now often referred to as "A Lost Generation."

Curtis imagined himself concluding in his editorial voice that, as Fairfield alumni move toward their 50th high school reunion, perusing the pictures and accounts of classmates in this commemorative book, they should see their coming together as a celebration, not just of what they had accomplished in half a century, but also of the good fortune of their upbringing.

He chuckled wistfully in recalling a childhood in which the only (recognized) minority were Roman Catholics, not members of racial or ethnic groups. Still, there had been half a dozen black classmates in a total of 180. Had there been segregation in Missouri, he asked himself? After all, it had been a slave state before the Civil War.

If so, he wondered where did those black students in Fairfield go to school before the 1954 Board of Topeka Supreme Court Decision? He could remember no black students in his classes until high school; but maybe they were in different classes. He would have to do some research . . . and ask his mother.

In any case, he would write the class that, thanks to their parents, they had always been a "Found Generation." And it is my hope, he would conclude, that, while we look back with some nostalgia at our high school years, we will also carry forward an understanding of how lucky we are, finding (as new founders) ways to contribute to the welfare of our grandchildren's world.

During Curtis' musing, he decided to make a nostalgic stop at The Hilltop, once advertised as the "world's largest roadside restaurant." On Route 66, it had served hundreds of travelers daily in its glory days. On his visit today he would have occasion to recall a future he had at one time contemplated—becoming a geologist—in contrast to the one he'd pursued as an English professor.

The Hilltop building survived now as a truck stop and convenience store for small towns in the area. Its original beige brick structure—with one end of the long building rounded and featuring floor-to-ceiling windows side by side—was easily recognizable. The Lindblooms had stopped there on trips east.

Today the old Curtis needed to use the men's room, and the younger one wanted a pie of pie. So, despite having eaten a sandwich at a drive-through an hour earlier, he sat on a counter stool and considered the menu's assertion that their apple pie was homemade and "better'n anything 'cept what your mother baked."

He ordered apple pie with coffee and then scanned the restaurant's interior, decorated with cores of old advertisements for gasoline stations, motels, ice cream stands. He also smiled at an imitation of one of the Burma Shave slogans on the wall. Along an artist's version of Route 66, successive small signs spaced a tenth of a mile apart cautioned: "The road's an open book. / But be sure to look. / Seek the end / that's your friend. / Jesus."

A man on the stool next to him was absentmindedly tapping a folded piece of paper on the counter. Curtis caught his eye, and they nodded in a friendly matter. Then Curtis said, "Excuse me, but it's Roger, isn't it? Roger Boyd. I'm Curtis Lindbloom, and I got your bio and picture for our class reunion just the other day."

"Hi!" the man smiled, tucking the folded piece of paper inside his jacket pocket. "Yes, and I might have recognized you from the sample entry you provided. You're in North Carolina, I thought, so what brings you here? Reunion's in the fall."

Curtis explained and then asked if Roger were headed for Fairfield, too.

"No, I'm meeting some other geologists down in Ironton, USGS old-timers' get-together." The Midwest office of United States Geological Survey (USGS) was headquartered in Fairfield. Curtis remembered that Roger now lived in Missouri's Bootheel.

"I guess that's a good place to meet, in the St. Francois mountain range."

"Interesting that you would know that."

"Well, yes, I've been an English teacher all my professional life, but summers in my college years I worked for the Missouri Geological Survey. And, in fact, the first summer, I went with a USGS team to North Dakota. So, any others you're meeting from Fairfield?"

Roger mentioned five, and Curtis recognized the names but remembered almost nothing about them. Roger explained that they'd been a bit of a clique in high school, the rock hounds--"not a music group," he joked. Growing up in the country, they played and worked outside, which may have led to their interest in geography. They retired to this area because of their appreciation of landscape.

"You were all in 4-H?" Curtis asked.

"From the beginning. Summer camps, clubs, regular family events. It was a different circle from you guys headed for college."

Curtis was embarrassed that his friends—and he, too—had looked down on classmates wearing the blue corduroy 4H jackets who sat together in the cafeteria, gathered behind the building before and after school, took vocational courses like shop and mechanical drawing.

"Many of you end up in the military?" Curtis asked, hoping for common ground.

"All the fellows I'll see today did. Yeah, most of us were drafted after high school but came back to find work at the Survey. Well, all but one. We started out in the field because we knew the outdoors and didn't really want to work in an office."

Roaming through his childhood woods, Curtis and his neighborhood friends had often combed creek beds for stones in interesting shapes, frequently claiming to have found "Indian" arrowheads, hatchet blades, spear tips. The dominant rock is soft limestone; but harder flint is abundant also, and they sparked fires in dry grass by striking those stones with a metal object.

Could he have made a career in the Survey? He'd always

appreciated his biologist wife's connection to the material world of plants and animals, as his own profession of letters tended to encourage people to live in their heads, vicariously.

Seeing Roger check his watch, Curtis slipped off his stool. "Well, this was interesting. I hope your friends are planning to attend the reunion. I'd like a chance to learn more about your careers. Even in the Army, they made me one of the vast clerical class, pushing papers and having them push back against me. It fit in with my studies of writing."

That he spent all his time in the military bureaucracy didn't give a complete picture of his experience. His assignments in Vietnam had him interviewing soldiers in the field from the Mekong Delta to the coast of the South China Sea and up in the central highlands.

Roger handed him a card with his phone number "If you come back this way, let me know. I've got an interesting story about a veteran I'd like to share with you." He took the folded paper out of his pocket and held it up to suggest the story was written there.

When Curtis did hear that tale, he reaffirmed his plan for *Confluence II*: an appendix of those who'd served, when and where.

Chapter Thirteen: Gags

Although he feared the crust was store bought, not made from scratch, the pie was good enough to justify Curtis' checking off one more item on his Déjà Vu list: down-home Missouri cooking. Paying at the register, he couldn't foresee that over the weekend food would undercut Patrick's scholarship plan. He would have to combat a free lunch idea.

He got to the Midwest Mother Road Motel only a little

later than he'd planned and found a message from Janet at the desk: "When you get here, meet me at Hillbilly Shed next door."

They'd reviewed travel times by email, thinking it might be wise to go over their scholarship strategy ahead of informal talk at The Table and more official action the next day. It also amused him to think he might find a gag gift for Beth at the gift shop.

"I like secret meetings," he joked when he found her eying Show Me products like the Missouri Weener Kleener (a block of wood with a hole in it), the Hillbilly Bank (a sock), and the Ozark Boob Kit (two balloons).

She smiled and gave him a hug. "We are, you know, co-conspirators."

The idea amused him. He wondered if her friendliness might be a welcome instance of his identity in the class being reevaluated.

Janet turned back to the shelves she'd been examining. "I love coming in here for the goofiness of it all, but they sometimes have some fine local craft items—braided rugs, knitted shawls, wall hangings."

"Ah, your line of work—weaving. Not sure I'll find literary masterpieces here myself, but I might as well look before I go. And as we browse, I'm feeling you must have something to say about what's going to happen this weekend."

"I'm not sure exactly, but did you see the one email to the group about 'preempting the call for contributions'?"

"I did, but it didn't make sense to me. Contributions for what? Are you thinking it's part of a conversation we weren't supposed to be included in?" With a chuckle he took an item off the shelf in front of him. "Now, this takes me back." He showed her the "Butt Dump," a teacup sized, toilet shaped ashtray.

Janet admitted, "We tend to forget that much of our youth was passed in smoke-filled rooms—at home, restaurants, college classrooms."

Many of their generation's parents were smokers, and public facilities and most homes had a least one ashtray somewhere. Some commemorated places visited (like Hannibal), events in their lives (25th anniversary), homes of famous people (President Harry Truman). But there were also other somewhat off-color items that had a place in Hillbilly Shed.

Curtis admitted, "My Mom smoked, but moderately. Now, my Dad . . . "

"Tobacco is history in this country," asserted Janet. "But we have new American vices like fast foods. People no longer plant gardens, cook, put up fruit and vegetables. It's another of those two steps forward, one back—or the reverse."

When Curtis and his siblings had to clear out their parents' home after their mother moved to North Carolina, he was struck by how strongly the smell of tobacco permeated clothes, furniture, and carpets. It was an aspect of his past he tended to repress, powerful though it was.

They sat at opposite ends of a bench under the window, and Curtis said, "So, let's get back to a strategy for selling the scholarship fund. Patrick and I thought a few of us who could afford it would make sizable initial donations. Then, if we keep everything confidential except a running total, a lot of folks can make modest contributions without feeling guilty." He was thinking of how Betty said it was hard for some to find extra funds in retirement.

Janet picked up another item. "Now this is truly tacky." There was a postcard with the words "Ozar-Key" printed on one side. The back featured the drawing of an outhouse. There was no lock on the door, no key attached.

She shook her head. "It's amazing how America has always been able to generate new kitsch, often mocking our own regional traits. It may be the one unchanging aspect of our national identity."

Curtis realized the Hillbilly Shed didn't need to be redone to fit into the 21st century. Its merchandise continued the same stereotypes in new media.

Reflecting on the mysterious email, he said, "Hmm, 'preempt.' Well, my idea was to try to speak up early tomorrow anyway. Do my own preempting."

"That sounds good. You're obviously a veteran of department meetings."

"Oh, yes. I'm going to exaggerate a bit and announce that we're already at $500.00."

"I can do my share. I'm not going to push Betty on it, of course." She had driven down with Janet, and they shared a room at the motel. "I'll see if I can corner Jimmy at the Table. He's the mayor and had always been civic minded. He'll see this as a good community gesture."

Curtis imagined a headline in the *Fairfield Daily News* (assuming it still existed): "'Graduates Grateful Half a Century Later.' He told Janet, "I'll talk to Gary tonight, too. It turns out the Vietnam vets form a subgroup of the class. If I can get him to lead, others might follow."

"Okay." She paused. "On another matter—how's the mini-reunion idea going?"

"Now, that's an interesting question. But before I try to explain, I need to get this." He held up a slim volume, *Dirt on my Shirt*, a children's book by hillbilly expert, Jeff Foxworthy. Curtis and Beth were waiting for a grandchild, so he could add it to the box where they stored future presents. The subject matter would be only mildly irritating to Beth.

"Give me the short version of the bridge party story," Janet said as they moved toward the cash register—also decorated with miniature outhouses, whiskey jugs, and girls in pigtails, They wore shorts and men's dress shirts tied at the bottom and unbuttoned halfway down the front.

"Hmm. Well, Bill asked to be 'kept informed,' whatever he means by that. I'm going to see Cindy after Sunday. Let's say I have one weak hand but with some wild cards."

"You could tell Cindy, if she comes, that I won't show everybody the picture of her skinny-dipping in the Gasconade."

There was a basket of corncob pipes for sale at one end of the counter. She pointed and said, "This is another of those 'success stories' that has its dark side."

Washington, thirty miles west of St. Louis, was known as the "Corn Cob Pipe Capital of the World." The Missouri Meerschaum Company, "world's oldest and largest manufacturer of corn cob pipes," made the little town famous. The industry was a boon economically, but that success expanded the use of tobacco and its effect on the nation's health.

Curtis speculated. "I wonder if pipe making companies supported the tobacco companies whose research consistently showed there were no harmful effects from smoking."

"When some of my grandchildren were experimenting with cigarettes a few years ago," said Janet, "I researched the history. The Surgeon General's report came out soon after we graduated. We all ignored it, even though they printed those warnings on the packages."

"And yet we called cigarettes 'coffin nails.' We managed to keep that bit of wisdom disconnected from ourselves. It's the same with some college students today."

He recalled the little gift package Army recruits received at induction. They contained gum, a pocket copy of the New Testament, and several miniature packs of cigarettes—was it four smokes in each? If you didn't "light 'em up" on the day you went in, you probably did later.

Local legend had it that a Washington, Missouri, resident was the first to carve a pipe bowl out of corn cob. The friend he offered it to liked it so much that the carver moved from woodworking to pipe production, and an industry was born.

Successive improvements in manufacturing and distributing led to as many as a dozen more businesses sending corn cob pipes from Washington across the nation and around the world. When health scares about cigarettes soared, many smokers switched to pipes, believing them less harmful. So, it was more business for Missouri.

He couldn't say how many years pipe smoking had taken off his father's life . . . or how many his own dozen years of smoking—late high school, the Army, and through his graduate school days—might cost him. In the biographical statements he was receiving about deceased classmates, how many were smokers who died of lung cancer or heart failure?

They walked out of the Shed and crossed the parking lot to the motel.

As they stepped into the lobby, Janet said, "Listen: when we get to the end of the meeting tomorrow, I'd like to ask you a question."

"Okay."

"You can start thinking about your answer right now, though. Why, Curtis, didn't you ever me ask me out in high school?"

Chapter Fourteen: Blood

Although Curtis had hoped to talk up the scholarship at the Table, Tim Carlson caught him coming in and pulled him over to the veterans group. "You've got to hear this," he said. "It will put things in perspective."

"Crap," Curtis thought to himself, I can't seem to keep anybody on track here, either helping me organize the reunion yearbook or think about our legacy.

Tim nodded at Sandra, who was beginning a story Tim must have heard before. It would remind Curtis that, although his classmates shared a common past, each had a long personal history between their school years and the present.

Seeing the nod from Tim, Sandra began. "So this guy came to give blood the other week."

An Army nurse who'd volunteered for Vietnam and then stayed in the military for thirty years, she'd recently retired to Tarkio, a tiny town in the very northwest corner of the Show-me State. In her *Confluence* bio, she claimed life was clean and simple in this community of 1500 laid out in a rectangular grid on flat prairie land.

"You must not be fully retired," Gary said to Sandra. "Volunteering?"

"Yes. But unlike many in the class, I've kept in the same profession."

Curtis knew that Tim, for instance, had run a business supply company in Kansas City but now made money as a professional poker player, traveling to Los Vegas once or twice a year and, apparently, doing quite well for himself. And, as Sandra helped the Red Cross with blood drives, he volunteered for and contributed to good causes in his area.

Sandra went on. "So, there was this guy on one of the beds, the bag on the side filling with blood, and one of those super-sized drink cups balanced in one hand. I was moving from donor to donor as the supervisor, and I heard him say 'Bubba, bubba, bubba, bubba.' Or at least that's what I heard."

Curtis offered, "I can't guess what he thought he was saying."

"You'll find out, but it was interesting that, when he spoke, it was with a kind of a lilt, a rhythm, sing-song. When he said it again, though, I heard words."

"Progress," asserted Jimmy,

"Yes. But I also learned why I hadn't heard him correctly the first time; he, I realized, had no teeth. His lips and gums were just smacking. But this time I could make out the words: 'Do you smell the cotton candy?' And, again, he almost sang it, "Do you smell the cotton candy.'"

Although only some in the group had not been listening intently at first, all heads were now turned to Sandra.

"Always the courteous nurse, I sniffed the air to see if, in fact, there might be a smell of cotton candy drifting from some far-off place. Tarkio is flat, and winds can carry smells from miles away."

Most in her audience nodded in assent.

"But I had to admit to the man," she went on, 'No. No, I don't smell any cotton candy.' And, looking more closely at him, I noted scruffy clothes, several days' beard, maybe a bit of a musty smell. And that cup he was holding? There were probably several hundred cigarette butts in there. He must have been combing the streets before he showed up here."

"One of those homeless men who donate every two months," offered Jimmy the mayor, who'd probably had to help make policy about vagrants in Fairfield. "We get them here regularly—money to fund a drinking binge."

The group nodded, aware of the high number of alcoholics among veterans.

Sandra smiled. "You'll like what he said next, though. It was, 'When you do,'—smell the cotton candy, that is— 'you'll know it's time.'"

Gary, an amateur student of religion, concluded, "What you had there was a would-be prophet, warning about the end of the world. 'Repent ye, repent ye.'"

Curtis agreed. "Yes, it's the old soothsayer's formula: the warning, an omen, foreshadowing (the smell of cotton candy means dire event to come)."

"Yes," Sandra said. "But a bit creepy. And the content (you'll know it's time) didn't add up, to me at least. I actually like 'Bubba, bubba, bubba, bubba' better for several reasons." She frowned and gave a shiver.

Curtis asked, "Why do you like that? It's just nonsense."

"Okay," Sandra sighed. "This is really a part two to the story. You see, a few months earlier, I was substituting at the ER down in Fairfax. And an Army veteran, just back from a difficult tour in Kosovo, was brought in by ambulance. With a baby."

"Oh-oh," said one of the group.

"What happened with them reminded me of a moment in 'Nam. But let me give you Part Three in the tale before that. And, hell, let's have another round."

Tim had already signaled their server, who was bringing two pitchers. When they were distributed, he said, "The floor is still yours, Colonel."

Sandra nodded. "So, I continued to go from bed to bed, and at one point I came to the refreshment area. As I'm sure you know, people have to sit for fifteen minutes after donating."

"And" suggested Tim, "your prophet was there telling others, 'Bubba, bubba, bubba, bubba.'"

"Yes," Sandra smiled. "But I must have been learning his language because I understood him. He was asking, in that same singsong rhythm, 'Do you have some Nutter Butters?'"

The group smiled, feeling part of the experience.

"Sometime later that day," Sandra went on, "one of the other volunteers said to me, 'Did you know that guy who left? He sang back-up for a rock-n-roll band I've never heard of in the '50s? Or at least that's what he told me. Made all sorts of money from a couple of key hits, then enlisted for Vietnam."

Gary was surprised. "Really? When he had it made! That sounds like a tall tale to me. The guy was just a street person."

Sandra nodded. "Sounded crazy to me, too. But, what he also told the volunteer made me think it could be true. She said when he came back, he didn't want to live like everybody else, didn't see any point in it."

"Where's he been, then?" asked Curtis.

"Claims he just followed the open road wherever he had a mind to be." She paused. "If he really had a mind. There were a lot of drugs, too, in the 60s—here and over there."

Tim asked, "So, 'Bubba, bubba, bubba, bubba' was background music for some hit?"

"Again, according to what he said, for several hits. Something like 'boob-a-boob-a, blue moon,' something like that."

Gary was thoughtful. "You know it could be the meaningless refrain of repressed war trauma leaking out. I've read that a lot of vets are experiencing it more and more."

"Well," Sandra said, "there's even more to this. Remember the vet who brought the baby into the ER down in Fairfax? His wife had gone to work, leaving him to watch their six-month-old child. They took a nap together, and when the dad woke up, the baby wasn't breathing."

"Sudden Infant Death Syndrome?" offered Jimmy sadly. He explained to the group that in such situations the police have to come; an investigation is required. The baby--the body--has to be taken away.

Sandra said, "I promised to go with the child, to not let her out of her sight. But even as I rode in the squad car, the dead infant in my arms, all I could hear in my head was the mother back at the hospital keening uncontrollably."

Tim took a long drink of his beer. "You might as well finish the tale, Sandra."

"Yes," she agreed. "Some of you probably had similar experiences over there. I specifically remember a Vietnamese woman—given her age, likely a grandmother--holding a bundle out to me as I came onto base after R & R in Sydney. I was in uniform, an American, a woman. I guess she thought I could save this baby dying of malnutrition."

"The baby may already have been dead, of course," admitted Curtis. "That would make me say 'Bubba, bubba, bubba, bubba,' for many years."

"What she was saying to me, though, was what I heard in my head for years after I came back. And I still hear it: 'em bé, em bé, em bé, em bé,' the Vietnamese word for baby." Curtis thought he would hear it now, too, underscoring all the losses they shared then and since.

Chapter Fifteen: Melons

In his room, Curtis asked himself who he should have asked out in high school. He had certainly thought about Janet, but she belonged in that comfortable social set who seemed always to have a current love interest. So had Betty—well, for her, there was that one particular beau.

Curtis had had one or two dates with one or two of the girls who make the homecoming court, who hold class offices, who are always in on the planning of school events. But no romance ensued. He sometimes blamed an older brother who was more interested in studying than dating and an abstracted father who provided no guidance on how to make the transition to "going steady."

As if she were eavesdropping on his thoughts long distance, Beth called on the telephone. "So, I thought I'd better check to make sure you're not planning walks in the woods with your old girlfriend Kathy Fahr."

"Not a bit. I'm back from the Table, and Kathy wasn't there. Maybe if she had been, I'd made more progress with the scholarship idea."

"Still facing resistance?"

"Well, it's more that conversations keep taking us off on tangents, everyone riding his or her own hobby horse, generally into the past."

"I can understand that. I have, in fact, a husband with a tendency to travel that way."

"Hmph," protested Curtis. "No more than others our age."

Beth went on. "What I'm about to report may encourage you in more backwards journeys. Mom told me that there was a black elementary school on Elm Street, and that you would know where that is. For all she knew, it might still be there. The building, that is."

"I don't know of any old school buildings in that part of town. Still, maybe a discovery about Fairfield history will provide reasons to commit to the scholarship as a recognition of the past. I'll certainly drive down Elm tomorrow on the way to the meeting."

He paused, then asked: "By the way, does it make any sense to you that I wasn't the most desirable boy in my class?"

"None whatsoever. Are you asking me to figure out how such a fantastic date was overlooked in his high school years?"

"I could be. I mean, I'm the same guy, only older."

"Times change, and a new era makes different people more—or less—attractive."

"Okay—I was a man from tomorrow back then. And today

I'm a man from yesterday."

After he'd hung up and gotten into bed, Curtis realized such revisions of his adolescence were confusing his sense of a linear shape to history. And that brought him to the old question: was it the journey or the destination that mattered?

Goal-oriented, he'd believed in completed projects, finished products. But at a stage when he was continually reflecting on how he'd gotten where he was, he gave new credence to the value of process, which was often circular if still forward-moving overall.

Throughout the reunion planning process, he'd enjoyed the discussions of possible celebratory events and the development of a second edition of the yearbook. But if both weren't successes, he feared neither the anticipation nor the realization would seem worthwhile.

And after the hints Janet had been receiving, this second planning meeting made him fear that the end of the reunion journey could undermine values that had guided classmates to this point in their lives. Perhaps more worrisome, he had to consider the possibility that he and the gifted friends of Castle bridge had been misled just like others, if in different ways. That he'd already been outmaneuvered by one group in his class became clear when it was announced that, over the winter, there's been discussion of a first ever "free lunch" reunion.

"We do this at our church," explained Samuel, who was a minister and director of a religious school in a small town fifteen miles north of Fairfield. "Every year on Columbus Day we invite anyone who wants to come to a watermelon feast on the church lawn."

"You have more than that to eat, surely," said Sandra.

They were meeting at Carol Yates house, a mini mansion on ten acres three miles east of town. Situated on a small hill, it had a 360-degree view of the rolling hills.

"Of course," confirmed Samuel. "We have grills going all afternoon—hamburgers and hot dogs. The ladies in the church have made coleslaw, pies, cakes, and cookies. It's our way of giving back to the community."

Curtis asked, "Of course, the reunion is a bit past watermelon season. Are you thinking pumpkins for us?"

Sam chuckled. "No, the idea is simply that we don't charge folks who come."

"You see," added John Robinson, "if the reunion dinner is free, we'll have a great turnout. What we do—those of us who've been fortunate in life—we make contributions to an 'event fund.' Barbara has gotten a rough estimate of what it would cost, and a number of us think the reunion committee can carry it off."

He gave a self-satisfied smile. Curtis knew he'd been quite successful as cell-phone pioneer, perhaps the wealthiest member of the class even after his three divorces.

"See," chimed in Sally, "if each of us comes come up with $50.00, we'd have it covered. Well, we'll need a bit more for a DJ, but, still, . . . "

Curtis understood. If they funded the dinner and the entertainment, they'd be able to say they would have to pass on the scholarship idea. That would be out of reach. But the sense of having "given back"—even if it was to themselves—would ease their conscience.

Similar reasoning had at times prevailed in his own church, as some parishioners termed projects like shipping their old books overseas "community outreach." Theirs was not an evangelical church, organizing mission trips to other countries. But sometimes they put together packages of food or clothing that were taken by larger organizations to areas struck by disaster. Personal involvement with people in need was rare.

Barbara turned to Curtis and asked, "Did you get an estimate on printing costs?"

"I think I can get copies for about $5.00 apiece." John said, "It would be nice if we could provide each person who comes with a copy. If we really want this to be a cost-free event."

Curtis calculated that perhaps as many as 70 to 80 individuals might attend: this would mean another $350.00 to $400. Goodbye, scholarship!

He and Janet commiserated at the $7.00 a person lunch buffet. She noted: "We're talking about $1,500.00 in contributions to pull off a free-lunch reunion with free yearbook. That knocks our idea of supporting a member of this year's class pretty much out the window."

"We're pretty good at feeding ourselves, though."

He surveyed the well-stocked buffet tables, which even included vegetarian options. Fried chicken, of course, a pasta dish, steamed vegetables, a variety of breads, fruits, pie and cookies for dessert. At a separate table, coffee and iced tea, soft drinks, bottled water, were artfully displayed around silver bowl of ice.

Janet chuckled. "We're not in the 1% of rich Americans, but we're above the poverty level. Certainly Carol Yates is—what do you think her place is worth?"

"More than a million at least. It's not one of the two-bedroom houses most of us grew up in. But this reminds me: my mother said there was a black elementary school in Fairfield when we were kids. She said it was on Elm Street. I drove over there this morning and didn't see any school building along the way."

"It's a church now. They added a larger chapel to the original building, so you wouldn't recognize it as a school. But, yes, until 1954 the few black families of Fairfield—and I guess Phipps County—sent their children there. At least until eighth grade."

"And then . . . ?"

"I'm not sure. You'd better Google it—try 'Negro Schools in Missouri' before the Brown versus Board of Education' decision."

After the session Curtis would find the church on his way back to the Midwest Mother Road Motel. No marker designated its history: how many children attended; how many grades; how many teachers, if more than one; what brought these families here in the first place? And where, by the way, did they live?

A chasm in the picture of childhood had opened. And Curtis feared filling that space would add to the dismantling of other memories.

Chapter Sixteen: Fireworks

Curtis and Janet agreed that the scholarship initiative had taken two steps back from the one step forward they'd anticipated and that a major reset would be needed. They decided to keep a low profile for the rest of the day and talk to Patrick later.

The afternoon agenda (meals, mailings, decorations) created few disagreements, though Curtis did have some reservations about the patriotic display proposed by Barbara Lemon.

"We can put up a 'wall of honor' for the veterans in our class," she proposed. "I'll add a note in the next mailing asking for old photos of our men and women in uniform. I'm assuming Curtis," she smiled at him, "can pass on information about branch, years of service, tours, and so forth, so we can annotate the board."

"Shouldn't be a problem," he said. Since he'd set a strict limit (700 characters including spaces), he focused on family and careers in his draft bio. He would have to change that.

"My daughter has agreed to use the photos to make a slide show," continued Barbara. "It can run in the background throughout the evening."

"That's perfect, agreed Sam Peters. "We can intersperse those pictures with images from the old yearbook, as well as the ones people are sending in."

"And, of course," added Barbara, "we'll play the national anthem at the big dinner, and John has a good idea about taps."

He confirmed. "We've got two trumpet players, so echo taps—one at each end of the hall—will be great to remember all the members of our class who have . . . passed on."

John Robinson mused. "Earlier, I thought we might post the colors of the different branches of service—you know, Army, Navy, Air Force, Coast Guard—but that can take time and we want to socialize." Curtis did not think John had served himself.

Janet raised a hand to ask about table decorations, for which she and Betty had volunteered at the last meeting. "Will you want a patriotic theme there? Little flags, red, white, and blue paper plates and napkins, stars and stripes tablecloths —that sort of thing?"

Curtis thought he saw her give him a slight wink. Was she being ironic, hinting they might be going overboard?

Tim Carlson said, "If you do that, let me know. I've got contacts with a supplier of party favors. He's got coffee and soft drink cups, engraved pencils and pens, decks of cards."

"It's our 50th," explained Carol. "We should go all out. Remember, some of us were from military families stationed at Fort Leonard Wood, and all our parents made sacrifices during World War II. Most of the boys in our class, inspired by their fathers, were in the military."

Sandra observed, "Well, there was a draft for our generation's war." Her tone suggested she didn't view the Vietnam War as a grand cause like the earlier campaign.

More brightly, Carol piped up, "Hey, everybody loves fireworks. And I've contracted a professional to put on a show out at Fairfield Park after the end of the Friday social hour. They still have them every year there, you know."

Curtis remembered. The show was in conjunction with a traveling carnival.

He didn't, however, like the fireworks he witnessed in his adult life, which seemed to him excessive. People in his area made special trips to South of the Border, an over-the-top roadside attraction just over the North Carolina border. It featured restaurants, gas stations, video arcades, motel, adult shops, and multiple firework stores. Folks came home with car trunks full of firecrackers, black cats, M-80s, lady fingers, smoke bombs, fountains, sparklers, poppers, snakes, roman candles—the works.

He cautiously raised a question. "Are you sure we're not overdoing this a bit? I mean, I was in the Army like many of you, and I appreciate shows of support. But our class served the country in lots of ways: teachers, business owners, doctors and nurses, construction. I'd like to congratulate everyone on what they've done for the country."

There was a pause. And Curtis felt his observation was being greeted with the same lack of enthusiasm the scholarship idea had been.

Carol was the one to express what seemed a general sentiment. "Recognizing veterans happens all the time, Curtis. We love our country. And the rest of us know we're included in those events, which really do celebrate the contributions of all citizens."

The faces looking at him made it clear she spoke for all. Or most. Janet was looking down at the table, and Sandra's gaze went over the top of his head.

"Well, I'm happy to go along, too. Just kind of thinking about how our war, the Vietnam War, did more to divide this country than unite it. And we don't want to be reviving old injuries."

Tim nodded and said, "We can use the occasion to put that behind us, I hope, come together the way we were before . . . before that time." He'd served two tours with the Navy in Southeast Asia and knew the pain caused by clashes between angry protestors and gung-ho supporters.

Curtis had come to realize that when he felt others were unwilling to talk about the Vietnam War, he was sometimes projecting his own reluctance to confront that part of his past. He decided he would step back and let the group's feelings prevail.

93

The conversation moved on to the timing of more preparations and the agenda for the summer meeting. Curtis caught Janet's eye. When she raised her eyebrows, he concluded that she would like to talk more about the reunion theme. He mused about patriotic events in his youth.

Most boys in town (and a few girls) saved their allowances or paper route earnings to buy fireworks and spent the day of the Fourth setting them off, with sparklers, roman candles, and a few rockets saved for the evening. Curtis enjoyed it like the rest.

He'd realized some years back that few used the term "Independence Day" to identify the holiday. It was as if the turning of the calendar, not some historical event, led to a day of fun in midsummer. He hadn't counted the number of fireworks displays he'd witnessed as an adult, but it seemed to him they were more frequent and grander in scope.

Curtis' pleasure in blowing tin cans set on the street up into the air, battling others for the highest rocket, and scarring sidewalks with snakes ended the moment he saw Jack Jackson, neighborhood bully, drop a smoke bomb with fuse burning down Willie Adam's butt crack.

Willie was seriously overweight and in the middle of a three-year growth spurt. So, half of the year his old pants were too small, the other half the new ones too big. Although he suffered the usual ridicule at school and at home, he was remarkably patient and never retaliated.

When he crouched (in his small clothes phase) to light a cherry bomb set in the end of a pipe, his pants were pulled down in the back exposing several inches of the gap between his cheeks. Intent on his own explosion, and used to getting kicks in his backside, Willie didn't realize what was happening until he felt the burning.

"Smoke ass!" laughed Jack, as Willie leapt up and slapped his rear. He didn't realize immediately that smoke bomb was inside his pants.

"Drop trough!" yelled Jack. "It's the mother of all farts. Put a cork in it."

Willie did drop his pants and sweep out the smoke bomb. But what he did next surprised us all. He dropped Jack with a single short punch to the head. Then he walked home.

The images stayed with Curtis—the smoking, the punch, the departure—and were recalled on Independence Day the year he was in Vietnam.

When it all started, he'd been walking with another Army reporter, Carl Jenson, from the latrine up to the bar that had been erected in the unit's barracks numerous rotations ago. Perimeter guards in bunkers and in the towers suddenly fired short bursts, and Curtis thought an attack was under way. But Jenson put a hand on his shoulder to stop him from running for a bunker and explained they were just celebrating the Fourth of July.

"Happens every year," he added. "REMFs [rear echelon mothers], many of whom haven't fired a weapon in their entire tour, gleefully open up with whatever is at hand. Even South Vietnamese forces in the area join in as if we were recognizing their own nation's liberation."

"Good to know," Curtis acknowledged. To himself he thought, "The mother of all farts. Put a cork in it."

Chapter Seventeen: Rubbers

On the way out of Carol's house at the end of the meeting, Curtis felt an arm slip through his: Betty was walking beside him. She said, "Janet told me you browsed Hillbilly Shed?"

"Of course. I'm sort of glad it's still in business, local character, know what I mean?"

"Jimmy tells me it's becoming a desirable property as the town considers a bypass from the old neighborhood out to the interstate." Curtis knew Betty had grown up on the other side of Piney Ridge, off the Circle technically but in the same general area on the west edge of town.

"Taking out the woods of our childhood?" Curtis said with an exaggerated sense of personal insult.

"I'm afraid so. But let me tell you about another of the kids from the Circle who roamed that area fifty years ago. His story might come in handy in your scholarship campaign."

Curtis hoped this meant she was changing her mind about the idea. Her tale, though, he knew could end up another detour from the reunion highway. Still, he leaned back against his rental Dodge Dart and said, "Fire away."

"You might not remember Bob Wheeler. His family lived close to ours, a little house at the end of the lane that petered out in the woods.

Curtis remembered the house—more, to his mind, a shack surrounded by leaning outbuildings, rusting car bodies, and always a pack of dogs. He stayed clear of the property. "Was he in our class?"

"No, the class behind. Bob went to work right after high

school at Sam's Tire Shop. He had to—no money for college."

"I know now—from the bios I get for the reunion yearbook—there were a lot that way."

Curtis also knew Sam's because his father had always bought tires there. The business was started after the war by an island-hopping Marine. Sam's reliability and fair pricing had customers returning year after year. He told Betty, "I know it was hot, hard work."

Betty chuckled. "Bob told me during that first year that he was turning into rubber. He had to pack defective and worn tires for eight hours a day. He reeked of rubber."

Curtis was beginning to think Betty and Bob might have been more than neighbors. So, this could be not just his story, but hers as well. He told her, "I went by the shop on my paper route. My job was a lot easier.

"Bob complained that Sam's was all tires, cars, and going places, whereas he circled from shop to home on a conveyor belt. Of course, they had conveyor belts in the shop."

When she paused with a pained look on her face, Curtis raised his eyebrows. She explained. "Later he would participate in this process of going in circles in a more tragic mode on the other side of the globe."

Curtis thought about the repeated efforts to secure rural areas in Vietnam. When US forces moved on from one area, the Viet Cong returned; and village life resumed in the old way. A deadly repetition. He asked, "So, Bob returned to Fairfield after his tour?".

"Yes, but there's a story within a story about Sam's. Tires were the primary business, but they also distributed condoms to local gas stations, the only source in those days."

Curtis remembered the ubiquitous machines mounted on walls of men's rooms. Insert a quarter in a slot in the steel knob, crank it once clockwise; the dispenser ate the quarter and spat out a Trojan.

Betty went on. "I wasn't exactly dating Bob back then, but we had . . . a special friendship. He told me once, 'I'm going round and around at Sam's. Pick 'em up at station 1, park them at station 2, retrieve them later as 'discard" (3) or 'repair' (to be packed, 4), return to 1.' I remember laughing and saying, 'Keep it up, and you'll be as rich or as round as Big Sam.'"

The shop owner's torso was spherical in shape and sat atop two short, sturdy legs.

"Funny thing," Betty continued, "he ended up distributing condoms in the Army, too, and back here when he worked for Martin's Tractors—'to protect farmers' daughters,' he joked."

Curtis observed, "My wife wouldn't like the joke, but she would approve of 'the prevention of disease.' Even with much more sophisticated birth control, too many youngsters today, it seems to me, follow the pattern of teenaged parents from the past, recycling ignorance. We need preventions against stupidity."

"Odd, isn't it? We have progress in some areas but are stuck in ruts in others. Bob would tell me about the new and better tire designs—tubeless, radials, self-sealing—each succeeding its predecessor. The new version also revolved around an axle of improved materials and design. But we had more deaths from automobile accidents every year."

He agreed. "Condoms, too, evolved. Before polyurethane products there was the latex condom, which came after the rubber that replaced lambskins."

"Oh, Bob kept me up on that evolution, too, assuming--wrongly—that I had great interest in what they went around."

Remembering she'd said that having an "older" husband pleased her, Curtis suddenly wondered if her interests went another way.

She sighed. "Something was going around and around in his mind. He'd made a bad mistake in Nam. Like many guys over there, he drank too much. And he was in a transportation unit, so he would go joy riding to blow off steam. He liked to spin his Jeep out on the beach. "

Curtis had known several from his unit who went from beer to other drugs. It seldom ended well.

"After he came back here," Betty said, "I would see him when he was home visiting family and old friends. He told me he could quit drinking any time, had, in fact, done it many times. They must have had a revolving door at AA just for him."

Curtis knew the syndrome and understood at least some of its causes. The only constant in Bob's troubled life seemed to be a downward spiral.

Betty went on. "At his base over there, there was a Vietnamese girl, Kim, who came seven days a week to wash the GIs' clothes. She believed, Bob told me, that if she worked hard for 'Joe,' she would escape the cycle of her ancestors' poverty."

"We left a lot of those behind," said Curtis sadly. "We saw them clinging to the helicopter skids in 1976."

"She didn't even get that chance. She was younger and more attractive than most, someone the men would fight over if she'd let them. Bob was . . . careless with her."

"Let me guess: no condom equals one baby?"

"Yes, but that wasn't the only disaster. A lot of GI's fathered children. It was another of his wild joyrides. I first thought only a vehicle had been totaled, not a Vietnamese national."

Betty explained that the girl lived a few weeks after the crash, the family unable to afford any kind of medical care. Bob was knocked back to private because of repeated instances of misconduct, but not discharged. Kim's aging uncle and aunt (the only surviving relatives) would receive modest (by US standards) monetary compensation.

"Bob, in a sober moment, went to visit," said Betty. "He found her lying on a pallet in their one-room hut on the edge of the jungle. He apologized over and over to her relatives. They bowed repeatedly but refused to take the money he'd collected from the unit."

"Whatever happened to Bob? He made it home to work for Martin Tractor."

She shrugged. "A few years later, one more joy ride. The truck cartwheeled across a cow field. No seat belt, so he somersaulted into a wood rail fence."

Curtis remembered a grim coming-of-age story from their teenage years. A drunken soldier on leave from nearby Fort Leonard Wood had driven head-on into a car carrying six Fairfield high school students to a band picnic. This was before seat belts were mandatory and when the concept of "drunk driving" did not exist. It was the first death of someone Curtis knew.

"Whoa! That's a sad story."

She leaned forward and gave him a hug. "We're not going to see many like this in the yearbook. Only those generally satisfied with their lives will send something."

"You're right." Curtis started to get in the car, but turned to ask, "I don't mean to be insensitive here, but I don't see a connection to the scholarship campaign."

"Bob was a good student, but, as I said, his family had no money. He was drafted the week of his graduation."

"Ah! A scholarship might have saved him."

While many individuals had been involved in this tragic chain of events, Curtis blamed Bob's death on one man, someone he had shaken hands with in 1967: Lyndon Johnson.

Chapter Eighteen: Deals

Curtis said goodbye to Betty, who, with Janet, was driving back to St. Louis. He would travel that way also to spend the night at his brother's and the following day head off to see Cindy. He and Roger, the geologist, had arranged to meet for breakfast before Curtis would drive up to Springfield, IL.

It was before Curtis left town, however, that John Robinson made his offer to fund the scholarship with two $5,000 donations if Janet would sleep with him. And Curtis surprised himself by agreeing to forward the proposal, in part, he realized, simply to get away from John.

John admitted, "I do have a second motive in this. I want to clear the table of this silly scholarship idea. $10,000.00

from an 'anonymous class member' will make everyone easier about contributing to the main party. And that's what I'm looking forward to—relaxed, probably a bit tipsy, nostalgic, fellow classmate."

"So you can make more conquests?"

John laughed. "That's entirely possible. Sandra's pretty hot, too, but I'm not sure she cares for men, know what I mean?"

Curtis did know but wondered if this man was reviewing the entire class for possible sexual partners. Curtis did ask a second time, "Why don't you make the offer directly? I don't see the need for a middleman."

"I see the way you two get along. In fact, I've been wondering if you're not interested in the same thing I am."

Curtis sighed. "I don't do that sort of thing. And if I did, would I be helping you?"

"But you are after her?"

"No, no. Believe it or not, some of us have marriages like our parents."

John laughed. "They weren't any more monogamous than we are. And some of us aren't paralyzed below the waist either." He waved goodbye.

Before starting to drive, Curtis made two quick phone calls: the first to Cindy Martin saying he felt he was on time and would arrive at her house in Springfield before noon on Sunday. He was going to make his case for Castle Bridge and then drive back to his brother Louis' house and fly back to North Carolina the following day.

The second call was to Janet to relay the bizarre conversation he'd had with John Robinson, wanting this issue off his plate and on hers. He made a third call that night from his brother's house, this one to Beth to he could recap the day of surprises.

"You're not making this sex for scholarship funds thing up, are you," she said dryly.

"I wish I was. I'm sure Janet can take care of it, though. She's no doubt had advances of this sort before . . . though not with so much money involved."

"I guess," Beth mused, "we've just closed our eyes to this sort of thing. But I'm don't believe our parents were so promiscuous. It's birth control that disconnected sex from reproduction. When was that exactly?"

"My first awareness came in college when a friend's girlfriend was in the hospital for a blood clot. He explained that it was not uncommon with the pill."

Beth sighed. "A huge benefit in one way for women, controlling their own bodies. But it came with complications."

"You know," Curtis concluded, "I got to thinking during our afternoon session that it might be fun to create a model of Fairfield in our basement. I could integrate it with the old model railroad that we stored in the attic. I would sanitize the set-up a bit, though."

"Don't you want it to be authentic," asked Beth, "an accurate representative of the past?"

He sighed. "I'm learning the past isn't as clean as we'd like to remember." He paused. "Say, I could put the train board on top of the snooker table."

They'd put a used 10-foot-long table, another of his retirement obsessions, in the dining room since they ate all their meals in the family room looking out over the water.

"You'd cover up your favorite good-old-boy pastime?"

A few of the veterans he'd gotten to know in the area would come by about once a week to play a couple of games and reminisce about their experiences; but that had been occurring less and less in recent months.

"You and I don't play anymore. If it were a model train set-up, you, a train lover might not complain so much."

Beth did like trains and had never seen the attraction of the smokey pool halls and greasy diners Curtis recalled fondly from his college years and his stateside time in the Army. She remembered such places from her childhood as smelly and dirty hangouts for boys with duck tail haircuts, T-shirts with rolled up sleeves, cigarettes tucked behind ears.

"Are you going to get out all your old matchbook cars?" she asked (perhaps satirically—he couldn't tell).

"Hey, that's an excellent idea!" They'd also been boxed up and stored when they moved to their retirement home after more than three decades in central Virginia.

Beth's sigh was audible on the phone. "Well, I'm going to let you think about all this as you drive about your Midwestern countryside tomorrow. It seems to me you have quite a bit on your plate already in writing a book about Route 66 roadside attractions, negotiating the reunion yearbook, completing the Lindbloom family saga, and planning a bridge game with only yourself as a player."

He knew she was right: he'd not get to building a miniature replica of Fairfield anytime soon, if ever. But he liked the feeling of order such a model might give to his sense of life's journey. As he lay down in the bed, he remembered Betty's story of Bob Wheeler, doomed distributer of rubbers, first as a teenager, then a young Army supply clerk, and later a farm equipment repairman.

"What my model town would need," Curtis laughed out loud, "is miniature condoms!"

In his imagined recreation of Fairfield, he visualized an updated model gas station run by an immigrant family. He saw condoms smaller than rice grains openly displayed in the glass case by the cash register rather than hidden in dispensers in the men's bathrooms. They would fit right in along with popular contemporary magazines featuring provocative pictures of semi-nude male and female movie stars, "natural remedies" for erectile dysfunction, libido boosts for middle-aged women.

Would this be, as Beth claimed, "sanitizing" the past or the future?

Chapter Nineteen: Invisibles

Curtis met Roger at America's Main Street Diner in Kirkwood. He had time for one of their famous breakfasts—Roadside Waffles—and to hear Roger tell his story.

"It starts," Roger said, "with Hidden Acres, a campground along the route of my many years' commute from Cuba to Fairfield. Funny name isn't it? How is someone supposed to find something that advertises it's hidden?" He stirred a teaspoon of sugar into his coffee.

"But I learned to appreciate that name when I realized how many things are, in a sense, 'hidden' right before our eyes. For instance, has it ever occurred to you as strange that the photos of houses in real estate ads are always taken from the street?"

"No," answered Curtis. "I guess that's just the way it's done."

"Yes, but that's not giving the potential homeowner the prospect he or she would enjoy if he purchased the house. It's the view others would have of the buyer's new home— that of the outsider, not the insider. Wouldn't it be better to offer the purchaser a picture of what it would be like to live inside this house, not outside it?"

Curtis chuckled. "I see your point. We are a culture of voyeurs."

"To be sure. And to put it another way, we study how we want to be seen in real estate ads, commercials, magazine spreads, book covers, real estate adds. But our attention is directed away from other things that are perhaps more meaningfully 'there.'"

He was sounding as much like as academic as Curtis did.

"I think I understand," he told Roger. "What's hidden in these ads is living room, bedroom, kitchen, etc.—all inside."

"Exactly. Also hidden, of course, are the leaky roof, the creaking stair, the out-of-date wiring."

Roger pulled a folded paper from his pocket and held it in one hand. Curtis thought it could be the same one he had held the other day at the Hilltop Restaurant.

Roger went on. "Here's an example of how we do this to ourselves without realizing it. I had for years two regular jogging routes: summer and winter. In both it turns out I blinded myself to an entire house."

Curtis asked, "You were looking the other way every time you passed?"

"You might say that I saw it and didn't see it. From April to October I used to run through my neighborhood and then out on a country road, passing a few scattered houses, cows, fields. The last house on my way out of town on this summer route is a small brick home. Its modest front stoop, wide dining room or living room window, small kitchen or bath window face Oak Street. I have always imagined two bedrooms and a bath behind them."

Getting into the spirit of Roger's tale, but drawing on his literary interests, Curtis asked, "Something hidden there? A secret gambling club, a moonshine factory, a madame and her 'girls.'"

"It's not as dramatic as that, but, yes, there is something hidden. I need to say that Oak Street has large lots, and back yards of the houses are bordered by Elm Street. Okay, now I need to describe my winter jog to uncover what was missing on my summer run. From October to April, I turn off Oak one block short of that last little brick home and continue on my way in town, not out of town."

"So. some of the route the same, but another portion different."

"Right. Now, one day I looked at a little brick house on Elm and saw a front stoop, a wide window for living or dining room, a small window for kitchen or bath. How could this be? This was where the back of my Oak Street house should be."

"Were you confused about where you were and looking at a different home?"

"No. But how could the house on Oak have two fronts?"

"Omigosh!" exclaimed Curtis. "There are two houses."

"That's it. When I retraced my steps and realized--well, I knew it all along but had never let it take shape in my mind— that at the western end of that block there are two small lots/ houses back to back in the place where I had thought there was only one."

He unfolded the piece of paper spread it out before them. It had a sketch of the neighborhood he'd been talking about.

"Rather than being disappointed at this discovery, though, I resolved to celebrate the fact that my world had just expand- ed. I now had two houses where for decades there had been only one. There were also, as you can see, two front yards and two backyards." He laughed. "My world was richer than I'd ever known by one, once invisible house!"

"Still, no underground neo-Nazi party, pot-smoking hippie commune, militant religious sect with enough firepower and provisions to hold off the FBI for a month?"

"Not a one. Just another regular family, same as the ones all us of grew up in and of which we are now the next senior generation."

"But it's possible we've hidden the fact that there may be twice as many of us as we thought," concluded Curtis. "Du- plicates as far as the eye can see."

Roger turned his straw around and around in his glass. "Yeah."

Then he turned the paper over. Curtis noticed that the sheet had been folded in half and then in thirds, the way a letter would be to fit in a small envelope "Take a look at this and see what you think it means." Curtis read:

Roger That,

Good to hear from you. Brought back old times. Got to see the kids weekend before last. Wow, had they grown! Linda looks good, too, though I could see the strain my being there caused her. Still, I felt I had the right, know what I mean? Anyway, hard to say this goodbye.

I've got a new guy from the VA helping me. He knows the deal. Everything continues trés bien with me.

If you come up to Omaha one day, I'll show you around. I miss seeing you, even though it's been . . . what? a decade. Hug the wife and the kids.

There was a scrawled signature, "Charlie Dog," at the bottom.

Curtis frowned, "Military nicknames, okay. But this doesn't sound good."

"Right. Somewhere along the way we added the military alphabet code to Charlie. As you probably know, everybody gets renamed in the Army. I became 'Roger That.'"

Curtis didn't admit what he'd become. He studied the letter. "He's having a hard a time here—divorced, I guess, but getting counseling. What did you write back?"

"No response is necessary." A pause. "He won't ever read it."

"Ah." A pause. "I'm sorry."

"Right. This is a suicide note, but . . . but the clue to its meaning was hidden right here in front of me." He sighed. "Maybe I didn't want to see it."

Now Curtis sighed. "Instead of there being another one of you, of us—like the extra house you discovered—there's just an empty space somewhere in Omaha, Nebraska."

"And no one will discover the Charlie Dog I used to know, the one who survived the war but not the peace."

"What else did you miss in the letter, what's hidden here?"

He shrugged. "The trés bien was his code for Bến Tre, a village where bad things happened."

"My Lai kinds of things?"

"Something like that, though not intentional. Charlie has hidden what we saw there from everyone back here."

"Ah, so he was not 'very well.'"

"No. I thought it was odd that he used a French phrase, even a common one. It's . . . it wasn't like him, or conventional Midwesterners like us. But I overlooked it or looked the other way . . . or . . ."

"I would have, too," admitted Curtis.

Roger opened the door on the passenger's side. "Tomorrow." He explained' ? I drive to Kansas City where Private First Class Charles Oscar Golf, Mortuary Affairs Specialist (92M), will be buried. I will see my friend Charlie one last time."

Curtis took his hand and held it for a long time.

Chapter Twenty: Handshakes

Springfield, the capital of the state of Illinois, has two capitol buildings: the original Greek Revival-style building reconstructed in the 1960s, a National Historic Landmark; and the current French Renaissance and Italianate one completed in 1888. Barrack Obama declared his bid for the Presidency in the older building, which was also where Abraham Lincoln delivered his "House Divided" speech in 1858.

Curtis recalled his one face-to-face contact with a U.S. President: Lyndon Baines Johnson, who was touring the country to demonstrate our stability in the months after JFK's assassination. When he came to St. Louis, Curtis and a friend traveled down to stand outside the Chase Park Plaza Hotel, hoping just to get a glimpse of him.

In a scene that would never occur post-9/11, President Johnson, after meeting with local dignitaries inside the hotel, came across the avenue and waded into the sidewalk crowd to shake hands. He started perhaps 25 yards away from Curtis and his friend, who were sure he'd never get to where they were.

But he did. And Curtis reached up—at the same time as half a dozen people near him did the same thing—and shook his hand. To this day he almost couldn't quite believe it: he shook the hand of the President of the United States.

To be more precise, his forefinger and thumb managed to close on the flesh between President Johnson's thumb and forefinger. But he's said that it counts as a "handshake."

Curtis did not magnify the division of his high school class to the level faced by the nation during the Civil Rights era when Johnson was in office, nor certainly in the period leading up to the Civil War when Lincoln became the nation's leader. But he did fear, as he believed Obama did, that the same issues were now dividing America.

Reconstituting the bridge table of his youth remained a major goal for Curtis personally. Still, he hoped common ground could be found to unite those in his class who wanted to isolate themselves from the global community and those who wanted to reach across the boundaries of their own circle.

His old friend Cindy met him on the front porch and gave him a big hug. "It's so good to see you." She looked over his shoulder. "I thought you might bring crazy Bill Castle to pressure me into playing bridge in the fall."

"Um, no. I did talk with him, but he's a bit . . . eccentric these days."

"So I hear. But come in, meet my husband, and we'll talk over a cup of coffee."

Frank was a charming man, retired accountant for the state of Illinois. He excused himself after a brief introduction to let the two classmates reminisce.

"So," began Curtis. "You've heard my spiel. I won't even insist you attend the official reunion events. Just come down for an evening of bridge, remember old good times and talk about new good times."

"What has Susan said?"

"She's a bit hard to get an answer from—busy, apparently, running her own foundation in California. But it's early enough, I'm sure she'll come on board."

Cindy refilled her cup. "You remember my mother, don't you?" she asked.

This seemed to him a non sequitur. "Of course, probably the best teacher in our high school. She opened our eyes to the world outside of our little town."

"Well, she paid a price for that, and it makes the idea of coming back . . . unpleasant."

"Your mom taught for forty years here," he said. "And she won awards. My mom sent me clippings because she knew how important she was for me and my siblings."

"What happened came before we reached her class in ninth grade, but the effects soured her—and later me—for a long time." She paused. "You see, someone—or someones—in that town, I never learned who, reported that she had associations, dangerous associations, with Communists."

"I thought the McCarthy era ended in the mid-50s."

"Not everywhere. There were quite a few closet J. Edgar Hoovers in Fairfield at that time. Several teachers in the school—even one college professor, or so Mom told me—decided to leave rather than battle the underground rumor factory."

"Did someone think she was a subtly subversive teacher, helping the Soviet Union in the Cold War by teaching revisionist history?"

"Principal Roberts didn't think it was true, but he was making sure she understood the kind of things that could happen. Remember: my father was a lieutenant colonel in the Army at Fort Leonard Wood. Roberts worried that this might affect his career."

"My parents never knew," Curtis said. "It must have gone away somehow."

Even as Curtis said this, however, he remembered his mother referring to some "incident" involving the Martin family and Fairfield.

"Not only would my mother not resign, she demanded to have an audience with the school board immediately."

"Good for her. Bringing these issues out into the open, where people have to say directly what they are thinking, can be a way of disarming your critics."

Cindy laughed. "Oh, she didn't just ask for an explanation. She let them have it! It was years before she told me this, but she asked for the names of accusers, she demanded evidence of connection to Communist, socialist, Bolshevik, un-American groups or individuals, she showed her membership cards in professional and civic organizations."

Now Curtis laughed. "Her teacher's voice intimidated even the most rowdy teenage boys! The school board probably felt they were pupils rather than bosses."

Cindy nodded, but more soberly. "Yes, she won the day. And never even told my father about it. But to be under suspicion like that, when you were a dedicated public servant . . . it hurt, I can tell you that."

Curtis was putting together a timeline. "She taught here until retirement?"

"Yes. And then lived in a retirement home until she died, even though I wanted her with me in Springfield. She felt leaving would be giving in, admitting guilt of some sort. She was going to look the good citizens of Fairfield in the eye until the day she died."

"But when she did pass away, you decided never to return to your hometown."

She smiled. "That's right. But . . . the goofy idea of a rubber or two of bridge more than half a century after we got together many a Friday night is . . . appealing. In fact, I've lived a life here much like my parents. And my children had similar . . . goofy . . . pastimes growing up. So, what the heck! Deal em'.""

"That's great. And, again, feel free to skip the other events. I doubt if Bill will go to them either. And I'm not sure yet what Susan will do."

"Okay. But remember--I still want you to ask for school board minutes from 1955—I've written out the exact dates. Freedom of information acts require they turn them over, but I believe they'll be a lot more attentive to a request from you than they would from me. I . . . sort of have a history with them."

"I promise to write as soon as I get home. And I'll tell them I will be in town in July to demand them in person—with my lawyer at my side—if they're reluctant."

"Of course, the record may have been purged, but I want whoever has inherited power in that town to feel some pressure on matters like this. At the least, it might protect a teacher today who's falsely accused of not being a patriot."

Privately, Curtis thought this was a bit extreme. Still, he could see so much pain and anger in Cindy that he hoped this would allow her to put the matter to rest.

That Communism was threatening to take over the world in the 1950s and '60s one country at a time was a chief cause of the Vietnam War. That was when he (metaphorically) shook President Johnson's hand a second time when he opened the letter signed by the President that began "Greetings."

Americans now vacation along the South China Sea where

many US bases once were and visit Hanoi, the ancient capital of the country on which we dropped twice as many bombs as we had on Europe and Asia in the Second World War. We held on to worn out beliefs through the 1970s and beyond at the cost of more than 57,000 of our own lives and millions of others.

Could we claim progress as a nation if we didn't admit our mistakes and alter our behavior?

Book Three: Susan
Chapter Twenty-One: Respect

Back in his North Carolina home, Curtis bragged that, after the summer meeting of reunion planners, his chances of completing the Castle House Project were better than fifty-fifty.

"But you still need a fourth, right?" Beth insisted.

"Susan is, like some of our age, as busy or busier than when they were working."

"Of course, your mom could be a fourth. She's still playing cards at the retirement home, and she may be leaning toward making the trip to Missouri."

"I think she truly wants to go but has some legitimate worries about her health."

"Well, maybe this letter from a doctor will encourage her."

She handed Curtis a thick envelope with "Dr. Susan Howe" in the return address. He opened it and found four printed sheets. "Now this is interesting," he told Beth. "It's entitled, 'Why I've Un-retired.'"

It was, in fact, a narrative of her effort to shut down her medical practice and turn over the direction of her charity to her daughters. She included a brochure about Woman's Body, her foundation that supports female centered medical care. The focus of the narrative, however, was how a luxury vacation to exotic México undermined her efforts to curtail her life's work simply because she had reached a certain age. She wrote to Curtis about what this first retirement excursion meant in terms of her participation in the class reunion.

From Los Angeles we [Susan and her husband Warren]

sailed on one of the big cruise ships to Cabo San Lucas on the southern tip of the Baja Peninsula. There we played a few rounds of golf, saw dolphins in the Sea of Cortez, ate shrimp tacos from a street stand, and watched blue-footed boobies soar above fishing boats. We were doing what we were supposed to supposed to: getting away from it all on a dream holiday.

Puerto Vallarta featured more recreational opportunities, but with special escorts. One of our son's best friends from childhood, Jackson Barber, along with his wife, Debbie, welcomed us at the dock for the boat's 36 hour stay in the city.

"You need to get away from the tourist places for at least half a day," the young couple argued. "Let us take you to San Sebastian, a picturesque little village only an hour and a half drive from where we sit." He gestured vaguely to the north.

We had already toured the school where they taught, walked through the farmers' market, and shopped along the Malecón, a stone seaside walkway where artists built elaborate sand sculptures, strolling musicians entertained, and sombrero-wearing peddlers offered their wares.

Warren pointed out that we would want to take some things to our friends back home. And they knew prices in a little village would be much better than in the city. There was also, Debbie added, an old church worth seeing in the village.

They didn't explain that San Sebastian de Oeste, a former mining village, was in the Sierra Madres. There were steep mountains, switchbacks on the road that wound along sides of high cliffs, and ancient stone stairs. Since childhood I have had a terrible fear of heights.

I found myself in a battered Chrysler mini-van rattling along narrow roads (some cobblestone, some dirt) past smaller and smaller villages. Why had I assumed our destination would be along the coast, a comfortable drive north along the beautiful bay's shore? I'd been lured into acquiescence by margaritas, fish tacos, multi-flavored ice creams.

On the way out of the city we rode past a large working-class area, crowded neighborhoods where laundry was hung between buildings and the people raised chickens in common yards. It looked as if, whenever they had to accommodate more family, the residents simply added levels on their flat-roofed adobe houses. The population density had to be high.

Such conditions meant high health risks and made me think about our comfortable retirement.

We were still close to the ocean, so I didn't feel anxious about the hills I could see in the distance--until the climb began. On our way up the mountains I noticed workers repairing roads. Using picks and shovels, they were filling in washed out roadbeds on the rocky mountainsides. A fall from there would be deadly, I thought, and tightened my seat belt.

Jackson had talked a long time the night before about the difficult life of ordinary Mexicans. Those who could find work, hard labor or otherwise, were grateful. "When you see how tough it is to move up, even though the country has made a lot of progress in recent years, you can understand their desire to cross the border."

I told Warren that Jackson and Debbie reminded me of us in our early years of practice. We'd both been driven to rise in an increasingly competitive environment.

I had never admitted to Warren all the reasons that finally convinced me to retire. One of my patients, a young construction worker, not even twenty, had failed to hook his safety belt and fell through a church roof, landing face up on a brick floor. He survived but had to endure multiple surgeries and lengthy therapy. My aversion to heights exploded at the sight of Todd's mother bent over her unconscious son in a hospital bed.

I never thought my anxiety could be traced back to Vietnam's Central Highlands, where I'd served time as a nurse with a surgical unit. There were many facial injuries.

In the village of San Sebastian we were surprised to find an Italian restaurant just off the city square. The little piazza with lemon and orange trees, bougainvillea, and orchids was delightful. Above the rock wall we could see the steep incline of more mountains to the east and suspected the landscape here might resemble the host's back in the old country.

"So, how many people live up here?" Warren asked as we finished a splendid meal of lasagna and spinach ravioli (the owner made his own pasta), salads, and Noche Buenas.

"Maybe a thousand, but there are a lot of hideaways you don't see out in the forest ravines and along high ridges; some are virtual castles. It's close enough to Puerto Vallarta and Guadalajara that wealthy retirees own property here. And Canadian snowbirds come from cities farther up the West Coast mountain ranges."

"The roads are rough enough," I claimed, "you'd have to be careful coming and going."

"To the church!" announced Debbie gaily after paying the bill. (She had insisted it would be their treat, as she and Jackson were used to the exchange rate and the prices). She gestured down the narrow street to a steeple rising toward the sky. This was a cathedral, built when the gold, silver, zinc, and lead mines of the area had created a city of 20,000 inhabitants in 1900. The building was still the center of village life, its bell tower the highest structure in town.

"Look at the size of these doors!" said Warren. "It's not just how tall and wide, but they must be six inches thick."

We read that the building had been constructed around 1600 but rebuilt in the nineteenth century after an earthquake caused structural damage. All local material, as you wouldn't want to haul timber up these hills.

"The inside space isn't gigantic," noted Warren from the church doorway."

"What's this?" I asked pointing to a glass case with the life-size figure of a body lying on its back. It was nude except for some sort of loin cloth.

Jackson said, "A statue of the martyred St. Sebastian, pierced by arrows and bleeding."

The image bothered me, but not because I hadn't seen my share of dead bodies. I walked out to examine the exterior walls, thick like the doors. Gazing up at the bell tower, I felt dizzy. I looked down and saw a wooden sign with a carved message: "This house of God is not a museum; please drive yourself with respect."

"Check this out," said Warren, now standing beside me, to the others leaving the church. "Something lost in translation." He pointed to the word "drive."

I studied it a bit more. "I don't know. It may be something gained in translation. You know how many American church-es--especially mainstream ones like the Episcopal Church where we attend—are pretty casual about their Christian in-volvement in the world. We don't 'drive' ourselves so much as stroll and saunter along the way."

"True," admitted Jackson. One of the reasons we're here is to put our beliefs in practice."

St. Sebastian was not driving: he's lying prone in a glass coffin. And that's when I decided, not martyred and dead myself, I wasn't ready to stop working.

I'm even questioning whether I should take time off for a high school reunion. I guess you'll have to convince me. How about a Skype conversation?

Chapter Twenty-two: Mushrooms

Curtis was moved by Susan's reasoning. At this stage of life, most people were already in the process of reducing commitments. But, given current health care, they would likely live three or more decades with much of their energy and drive intact. Were golf, book clubs, vacation tours, nostalgic reunions enough to satisfy lifetime professionals? Beth had similar thoughts. And he suspected Patrick did, too; his friend was having a hard time giving up practicing law.

"Inequalities are on the rise, Curtis," explained Patrick in one phone conversation. "And I've got experience I bring to many cases my junior colleagues lack."

Curtis thought about that. "You know, we might use the argument that it's too early to give up on a number of issues to encourage Susan's participation in the reunion. She should see it as part of her commitment to continue building a better future."

"Listen, then, to my latest strategy to gain support: two scholarships, my friend. One for a male graduate, one for a female."

"Wouldn't that make our task twice as hard?" asked Curtis.

"In one way, yes. But if we say donors can designate which gender is to be a recipient of their contribution, we throw competition into the mix."

"Interesting," admitted Curtis, "Still, with the free lunch program already agreed on, we're ratcheting things up quite a bit."

"Well, not to overgeneralize, but men tend to respond to challenges. And nowadays, women don't shy away from them either."

Curtis thought about it a bit more. "Well, if we keep the class aware of the amount in each pot, we might be able to give two scholarships next fall. I say we see to it that the girls' fund stays slightly ahead of the boys', and some of our classmates might just find they have more resources in hand than they thought." He didn't say anything about John Robinson's offer to make contributions in return for special favors by Janet.

"You and I can get a base on the boy's side, and I'll see if we can get a major start on the female fund from some of the more prosperous women in the class. Tricia Bell's a likely sponsor. You also need to use your English professor skills to name this project—'Battle of the Sexes'?"

"Let me get back to you on that. But you've definitely given new life to the effort."

Thinking later about competition, Curtis recalled a mushroom farming experience from high school. Following a district competition, some of band members had toured a mushroom factory in Hermann, Missouri.

Band was one of the places where boys and girls competed openly for prestige in the '60s. The group marched in parades, performed at football games, and had their own concerts. Many of the girls had crushes on Mr. Clark, a former drum major at the University of Missouri. And the boys responded to the fact that he'd spent six years in the Marines. So, more of his classmates participated than in other schools of similar size.

Because chairs were decided by tryouts at the beginning of each year, boys competed against girls. Any student could also challenge the musician above him or her at any time. While women were excluded from the football field and basketball court, here they shared equal opportunity. And some, Curtis was to learn, reveled in the chance to best the boys.

He thought especially of Tricia Bell, who played drums. She was exceptionally talented and was in a local jazz band that performed at the country club, social fraternities, and in officers' and enlisted mens' clubs at Fort Leonard Wood.

At most performances Tricia was given a solo. The other musicians lay down their instruments to tap their feet and nod theirs heads as she played. She started slowly and under control but increased the tempo and the mixture of different drums, cymbals, and cowbell to rise to an intoxicating finish. The audience applauded, some standing to whistle and hoot.

Other bands were openly jealous of what she gave to the concept of march. Crowds at parades wanted to feel in step, but often couldn't even follow the varied punctuations of her sticks on head and rim. And when we were stopped for traffic, she broke the monotony of steady rhythm with improvisational explosions. We were okay musicians but spectacular marchers!

Every year Tricia was challenged for her chair by a series of boys. None came close to taking her place at the head of the section. Even at the time, Curtis knew she broke the mold of gender stereotype.

"You remember Tricia Bell?" Curtis asked his mother on one of her Sunday lunches at his riverside house. Mid came from her retirement apartment at least once a week for dinner with her son and daughter-in-law. She would often stay the night and have Curtis drive her back in time for lunch the next day.

"Of course. Lived on the other side of the Circle. Very nice girl. And quite successful. She started her own Joplin music supply company and had satellite stores across the country."

Curtis puzzled, "She didn't say anything about that in her yearbook entry."

"Her mother told me. You know, we were in the bridge club for many years."

Beth added. "Tricia is probably being modest in writing about herself, as we girls were taught to be back then."

"Apparently," said Mid, "Tricia showed her fire in the Miss Route 66 Beauty Contest. Her mother wouldn't give the details, but I think she had some sort of disagreement with one of the officials, and later he had to . . . remove himself from the program."

Hmm, thought Curtis, another possible class backstory.

That night he returned to his notes for the reunion yearbook and re-read Tricia's entry: "Happily married for 48 years to 'most handsome' [James Powers, so voted by the senior class], one grown child who has blessed us with three grandchildren. Still play timpani for the local symphony (and less formal drums in a jazz combo). Retired music teacher and devoted gardener in Independence Missouri." Curtis wondered if she cultivated mushrooms.

The band trip to Hermann, Missouri, some sixty miles west

of St. Louis on the Missouri River, had been memorable for many reasons: the glow of having won the regional marching contest (again), the raucous bus ride back home in the dark, and the mushroom factory visit.

Hermann was settled by German immigrants in the 1830s. The hilly terrain along the river must have reminded them of home, and a wine industry flourished there until Prohibition. For a brief period in the '50s and '60s one of the old wineries was converted to mushroom farming. The damp brick tunnels in the hillside created ideal conditions for fungus.

Wooden beds were stacked three to five high allowing only enough space between for the workers to harvest from the mixture of horse manure, hay, and corncobs. Mushrooms rise up overnight out of their beds (and in fields, gardens, and yards after rain) as if by magic. There is nothing there at the end of one day, then perfectly shaped plants are in view the next. Each time they are picked, explained the tour guide in Hermann, new mushrooms sprout in their place until the compost is exhausted.

The guide also described how their mushrooms were grown in darkness as fungi do not produce chlorophyll like green plants and need no light. It seemed to Curtis like a con-juror's trick, some invisible hand pulling strings in the dark.

Tricia Bell had been particularly interested in the process and asked questions about, among other things, the business' customers. Unlike today, fresh mushrooms were not common in family kitchens at the time but were primarily a canned product. This company sold to other businesses that processed and distributed their product.

Tricia was also among those interested in the close quarters and dark spaces of the mushroom factory. Rumors of who kissed whom circulated around the school for weeks. The best story was that Tricia backed future husband James Powers up against a wall, not only kissing him but shoving one hand down the front of jeans. Curtis chuckled that something besides fungi had sprung up in that darkness.

Matching original yearbook photos with new ones, Curtis felt some older selves had appeared for this reunion like mushrooms—overnight. Many a photo to appear in *Confluence* reflected a magical transformation—cosmetic surgery, dated photos, digitally enhanced images?

He studied the picture Tricia had sent and compared it to the earlier one. In addition to the mixture of language, tradition, energy that shaped them all—a society where girls were taught not to compete with boys—how had Tricia Bell, unlike so many, been produced?

Thumbing through other pages he also paused at the photo of Sonja Jones, the only black classmate to submit her biographical entry. Here was another subject for research, one that would likely reveal social dynamics that had been as hidden to him in high school. Which of his classmates would be willing and able to help him bring her story to light?

Chapter Twenty-three: School

There had been only ten African Americans in their graduating class, though Curtis knew others had attended for a year or two along the way. He regretted deeply that he couldn't remember interacting with any of them. As another goal for the early fall visit to Fairfield, he decided to quiz Barbara Lemon about those students' lives after high school.

Before he caught up with her, though, he had time to visit Liberation Baptist Church on Elm Street, which had been the black elementary school up until 1954. He'd come directly from the St. Louis airport this time, not stopping at his brother's, and checked in at the Midwest Mother Road Motel Friday afternoon. The usual gathering at the Table was several hours away.

He parked in the nearly empty lot behind the church and looked about for any historical plaques or other signs of the building's past. For all he knew, this was now a black church, and someone here might be able to fill in some of the blanks about Fairfield's racial history.

"Welcome, brother," said a large man who opened the door at his knock. "Baptist Union Baptist Church is never closed. Come right in and be welcomed by the pastor." He laughed. "That's me, the Reverend Abraham Lincoln Douglas."

It was hard not to smile back. "Curtis Lindbloom." He reached out a hand and received a stronger grip than he'd anticipated . . . or desired. This was a big man, well over six feet and perhaps 240 pounds. "Pleased to meet you."

"And I you. I wasn't expecting anyone, but as our savior told us, 'I was a stranger, and you invited me in.'"

"Why, thank you," said Curtis.

For many years he'd been embarrassed by open references to scriptures, as are many Episcopalians. But for various reasons, he'd become more comfortable with religious expression in recent years. And the man's open manner made him feel as if his private questions about the past would not be unwelcome.

Stepping past his host into the sanctuary's lobby, he explained, "I'm a Fairfield native come back for a visit. And I guess I was just curious about your church. I . . . I find every time I return there are sorts of new things in town, but also things I never seemed to notice as a child."

"Oh, we've been invisible in the past, my friend. Unseen and unheard. But not so much these days. We have a new president of these United States now, and those of us of the same color have, you see, popped out of the background." He laughed a deep open laugh.

Curtis smiled. "It's a good thing, if you ask me. But tell me about your past invisibility."

"I've got time; step into my study." He pointed to the open door on Curtis's left and preceded him to the other side of larger mahogany desk. Curtis noticed a significant limp, his right hip lifting up to bring that leg with him.

"Looks like we're both moving at a slightly slower pace than we might have a few years back," offered Curtis.

"God gives us only so many limitations as we can bear. This old leg got a bit shot up years ago, but it still gets me where I want to go." Again the laugh. "Steppin'!"

Although Curtis wanted to follow up on how Abraham had been injured, he thought it more polite to get to the reason for his visit. "You see, I'm one of a group that setting up a 50th reunion of our high school class. And one of the friends brought up the question of . . . of where black children went to school in the '50s. We don't remember classmates in elementary school, though there were certainly some by the time we got to high school."

Once more, the reverend laughed. "You see, 'invisible!' We were here." He waved toward the sanctuary. "We were right here. About twenty of us most years in three classes from grade one through grade seven."

"Ah, separate and not equal."

"My friend, you know of what you speak. Where do you live now?

Curtis tried to estimate how old his host was, wincing that he often found it hard with people of other races. Abraham had gray hair and beard, but even with the limp stood up straight and moved quickly. He guessed he might be ten years younger than himself—mid-fifties.

"In eastern North Carolina, but my wife and I spent our professional lives in Rural, Virginia, a significant place in civil rights history."

Abraham nodded. "They closed their schools."

Curtis offered a chuckle. "We had invisible schools, but visible students. Massive resistance to integration was before we moved there, but the shadow of those events continued to hang over the community and the schools where our children attended."

"Do you drink coffee?" asked Abraham, pointing to a small coffee maker on a table beneath the window.

A bit surprised by the non sequitur, Curtis still said. "Yes, though less at night now. Caffeine, you know."

"It's a generational thing: we all drank coffee, the office coffee pot going from 8:00 a.m. to 5:00. Our kids moved on to soda—Coke or Pepsi—but their children fill giant tumblers with energy drinks, sports drinks, things I don't even know about."

Curtis laughed his agreement, reflecting how he'd not always measured these cultural shifts as they happened. They were minor changes, he assumed, though he guessed scholars in some disciplines could connect the emergence of expensive coffees, lattes, frappes, the proliferation of ice cream flavors, and the varieties in design and color of athletic shoes to the spread of liberal ideas, the erosion of distinct gender identities, the explosion of new careers like "brand perception analysis," "aesthetician and skincare development," "project cost expertise."

"How do you like it?" asked Abraham, holding up a cup with "U. S Marine" printed on the side.

"As it comes." He felt to say "black" would be awkward, though he knew it shouldn't be. Then he asked, "You're a Marine?"

"Once and always. That's how I got this leg, jumping from airplanes. You military?"

"Army. The two-year career of a draftee."

"Hoo-ah," said Abraham and lifted his cup to Curtis. "But you wanted to ask about where we went to school back in the day. Until 1954, we were here for the first eight grades, but not allowed to attend the high school. So, we had to go up to Jefferson City."

"That's 60 miles away! You couldn't do that every day."

Abraham nodded soberly. "Most of the black children quit school then. Some found families they could stay with up there, but that was hard, too. And, interestingly, the school they sent kids to up there was considerably rougher than Fairfield. So, some tried, but gave up."

Curtis was trying to take this in. It was not as bad as closing the schools had been in Virginia, but similar. In Virginia white academies sprang up (like mushrooms) over night, so half the population continued their education. For the first few years it was in churches, converted warehouses, previously vacant buildings. Soon, however, permanent buildings were erected.

And the black children remained . . . well, invisible.

"I never knew. I'd like to get more information about this history. Are you the best person to ask?"

"No, I came along after we were allowed to go to Fairfield High. There is a man, Jefferson Brown; he's a resident at the nursing home, but still sharp. If you'd like, I can introduce you to him."

"I would like that. I'm in charge of putting together a reunion yearbook for our class and have considerable flexibility about what will go in. I have a feeling we ought to know about Lincoln School and its history. Would Sunday be a good time?"

"I think so. Why don't you come here for the 11:00 service? You can meet some of the congregation, and then we'll go together to the Manor. It's just out Highway 00 south."

Curtis felt he couldn't very well say no. "I'll be there. I'm in town until late that afternoon."

The reverend escorted him to the front door, a hand on his back, then shook his hand in farewell. Then he said, "Be sure to say hello to Patrick for me."

Curtis uttered a perfunctory, "I will," unsure if he'd heard right. His friend Patrick, author of the scholarship drive, knew this local minister? He staggered a bit out to his car, then turned back to wave at the smiling big man on the stoop. He'd have to ask.

Chapter Twenty-four: Skins

Curtis didn't call Patrick until late that night. "I've got one thing to tell you and one thing to ask," he said.

"Fire away. I'm winding down for the day." He still liked to argue in court and talked about retirement as vaguely possible in the future.

"First, do you know a Fairfield minister, Abraham Lincoln Douglas?"

Patrick chuckled. "Well, I haven't seen him in many, many years and didn't know he was a minister. His family moved to St. Louis, but the two of us spent summer days playing ball in Green Acres Park. He was a year behind us and one heck of an athlete. Went on to play high school and then, for two years, at the University of Missouri."

Patrick had played baseball in high school and college. "So the two of you kept in touch?"

"Not really. But our paths crossed again 'Nam, same unit."

"On the other side of the planet. That's some coincidence!"

Patrick sighed audibly on the phone. "Yes, but we weren't together long: he . . . was injured and medevac'd out of theater."

"Have you seen him since? Like the two of us," chuckled Curtis. "He holds his age well."

"No, but we do trade Christmas letters. Glad to hear he's doing well."

Curtis wondered why Abraham would know he was in contact with Patrick, but, again, decided to put that question aside for now. It could be as simple an assumption as, because he and Patrick had been close friends in high school, and there was planning for a reunion, of course there would be contact.

"Listen, I'm going to talk more with him, why he or his family came here in the first place and then why he's come back. It's part of our story I didn't know, black families in Phipps County. But I need to talk to you about another history in which we're more directly involved."

He could hear Patrick sigh on the other end of the line. "Blacks were a separate population back then. Except for the athletes, we didn't mix much at school. But what's up with the scholarship drive?"

"I don't think they're ready for the dual drive option, but I'll find out more tomorrow. I was just generally just trying to be genial tonight, not wanting to rub any feathers."

"Good plan. And by the way, I think Eddie Flanagan, a fellow Texan, is going to be there tomorrow. He might help your case."

Curtis didn't know Eddie well, but the yearbook showed he'd retired near San Antonio after thirty years in the Air Force.

He also reviewed the entry by Jones: "From Fairfield to Lincoln University (history major) to two years in the Peace Corps to graduate work (Washington University) to Kansas City where I met my husband and raised a family." She'd included a photo of, Curtis assumed, her husband and three children with their eight grandchildren—an attractive family. But this was a sparse account, and he decided he could solicit more from her, as well as from any who'd come short of the 750-character limit.

Curtis checked the directory (being compiled by Barbara

Lemon) and found Sonja's email address. He wrote and asked if there wasn't more she'd like to include in her biography.

At the same time, he proposed a Skype conference with Susan Howe. Curtis would be flying out of St. Louis early Monday and hoped the planning community would have given him reasons that would convince her to come.

Although he'd claimed to Patrick he'd been congenial at the Table, there was one exchange that bordered on confrontational. When he took a place near an end of the long table where about a dozen classmates were already enjoying each other's company, Curtis heard someone toward the other end say, "I'm telling you, we've got to take our country back."

Waving to the server and pointing at the pitcher being shared at his end of the table, he asked as innocently as he could, "Someone's taken the U.S. of A. away from us?"

There was a slowing of conversation, but it didn't seem as if anyone was going to answer him, so Curtis leaned forward and said a bit more loudly, "I'm serious now. I've heard this, you know, but I must have missed the theft. I'm in the country, paying taxes, about to start receiving Social Security, enjoying the land I grew up in. It's been taken away?"

Sam Peters asked, "You don't see the Spanish on road signs, at the bank, in advertising?"

"Sure I do, but English is there, too."

"People need to learn English if they want to be living in America. I've read they have Spanish kindergarten and early grade classes in some states. Before you know it, it'll be all the way to high school."

Curtis sighed. "You know I'm an educator, and I've read about this. When we provide avenues for children of other cultures to assimilate—like special language training in early grades—the great majority become tax-paying productive citizens. Especially in places like California and Florida, where farm laborers are essential to the economy."

"You and your brainy friends," Barbara Lemon huffed "might be able to learn Spanish and get along, but the rest of us are being pushed aside. And they take jobs that should go to . . . Americans."

"There've been studies about that, too, and the statistics show native born Americans are not taking low-paying jobs in construction, agriculture, factories. Businesses, in fact, recruit in Hispanic communities because they can't find enough workers."

"And I bet they use recruiters from México or some other South American culture," claimed John Robinson. "They speak Spanish and are not interested in finding English-speaking employees. Oh, they're taking over, all right."

Curtis was not willing to give it up but decided he needed to soften his approach. "I think you're right that the workforce is changing, but that's happened in the past—Chinese to build railroads, Italians to work in the garment factories of New York, German scientists who were crucial in building weapons in World War II." He omitted the Africans forcibly taken from their homelands to cotton plantations in the South.

Barbara responded, "But they all learned English, assimilated. Well," she chuckled, "I guess not everyone in China Town subscribes to *Time* magazine."

Curtis put a $20.00 bill on the server's platter as she passed behind him and said, "Let me get this round, folks." The server smiled and turned toward the kitchen. Curtis saw several in his group look up at her and frown. Curtis had seen she was dark-skinned, perhaps Mediterranean.

Even before he retired in the early 1980's, his father had complained that too many of the graduate students at South Central Missouri State were foreigners. "They're supposed to come here, get their education, and return to their own countries," he would say. "But they find life is pretty good in the U.S., and they end up staying."

Curtis would ask why the university accepted them in the first place and not get a clear answer. His dad admitted that most had high test scores and performed well when they got here. Still, he felt their English was not good enough.

"So, look," Curtis said, leaning forward to look down the table. "It seems to me about half of you here are women, and, in putting together the yearbook, I've been impressed by how much our female classmates have accomplished, what they've done for . . . for the nation, really We've got teachers, of course, but also nurses, and doctors! Some have started or taken over family businesses. Others went into local or state government. In a sense, they invaded the labor market I, at graduation fifty years ago, thought was only open to men."

He could see eyes looking down, some shifting in chairs. John Robinson admitted, "Yes, but . . . but they're . . . we're . . . all the same. They came with our values and traditions. It's still our country."

The faces in his group told Curtis he'd lost the battle. Except for one: Eddie Flanagan's. He'd kept quiet until now, watching the discussion with interest.

Shaking his shaggy head, he said, "I think Curtis is right. You all might not know this, but I met my wife in Texas. Her family's from México; she's second generation. Our children know more about what's going on in this country than . . . than most of us do. Plus, their mother's traditions. It's a double perspective, and they're the ones I turn to for advice."

How Curtis wished Eddie were a member of the reunion planning committee and would be coming to Sally's tomorrow!

Chapter Twenty-five: Drumbeats

The discussion that followed Curtis' dual-scholarship proposal increased Curtis' fear that, if there were to be a fund-drive, it would have to be outside the official frame of reunion. However, two surprise visitors gave him hope for an alternative path forward: Eddie Flanagan was there when Curtis arrived, and Tricia Bell crashed the party.

Carol Yates had tried to complicate the issue. "Maybe we need three drives—men, women, and . . . I hate the term, but . . . 'persons of color' because I don't know what it means."

She was a dark-complexioned woman who'd lived in Oklahoma until she was twelve; and in high school some boys had suggested she was what was then termed "a half breed."

While the Osage Indians had large populations in the Fairfield area early in the 19th century, wars with other tribes and encroaching European settlers drove diminishing communities west. So, there were likely very few or no Native Americans in Phipps County.

John Robinson supported Carol. "If we follow Patrick and Curtis' lead, we'd also have to have a scholarship for Hispanics, another for Indians . . . I mean, Native Americans. By the time we're 'politically correct,' we'll have dozens of scholarship funds."

Curtis thought to himself that this was a new version of divide and conquer. He looked around for help in the discussion, but even Eddie Flanagan was staying silent.

John, apparently sensing he had the upper hand, brought

up Route 66 as his example of true American initiative. "Route 66, now, America's Main Street, we don't partition it and give certain groups certain sections. It's quintessentially American."

He didn't say that the single, unified road was defined by whiteness, but Curtis felt the assertion was a subtext.

"Innovate entrepreneurs," John went on, "saw the opportunities a cross-country highway would bring to the nation, and they went about convincing state and local business to get on board. They found investors who would agree to sponsor related businesses. They didn't seek them by ethnic heritage but by ability to provide support."

Carol Yates agreed. "Places to stay along the route—hotels and motels—began to appear. Then, restaurants and diners with regular American food spring up everywhere."

Curtis waited for someone to insist that all of this was accomplished by "regular" Americans, not hyphenated ones.

He decided to interject. "That's interesting, but it's also true that women were involved from the beginning, not just men. They started businesses like souvenir shops with corncob pipes and corny postcards and clothing stores that featured cowboy clothes or frontier dress."

He didn't really know all this but suspected no one would challenge him.

His friend Janet Weaver added, "What we might think of as a Route 66 style—the design of billboards, motel room decor, gift shop displays—was very much influenced by women. So, I, for one, have to object to giving men all the credit."

Samuel Peters sighed audibly. "No one meant to exclude women, but the fact is men were the principal architects of national enterprise in the 1920s and 30."

Janet countered. "Quite true, but there were other movers and shakers of the time. When you have a chance, read about Sarah Breedlove, an architect in her own way. She invented and sold homemade hair-care products beginning in the 1930's and became a millionaire. And she should be included in the category of 'architects of enterprise.' And she was an orphan born to freed slaves."

Curtis smiled, aware that Breedlove's clientele were African American. He was pretty sure none of the men would know about this industry. So, he added, "Springfield, which claims to be the birthplace of Route 66, has this Mother Road festival every year. I was amused to learn that important venders include microbreweries run by descendants of German masters and taco stands that guarantee genuine Mexican tacos."

John groaned. "Here we go again—down the diversity route."

"Well, it's kind of hard not to, in my opinion. There's now a famous Route 66 motel—the Wigwam, I think, in Oklahoma or New Mexico—that's run by Indian Americans—that is, citizens of the U.S. who came from India. The times, they are a'changin.'"

"Agreed," admitted John, "though not all changes are for the better. What I'm saying here is that an important part of the past we're celebrating at this reunion involves entrepreneurs, men who made this country great. Think about the soldiers coming back WWII."

Eddie Flanagan, grandson of an Irish immigrant and married to a woman from Mexico, noted, "They have a Saint Patrick's Day event along Route 66 in the middle of Texas each spring. It's really helped a little town prosper. Irish-Americans have a way of contributing, too."

Saint Pat was the patron saint of Central Missouri State University, which many of Curtis' class had attended. So, that group—mostly men, to be sure—would understand the Irish impact on American life.

"Since they created the 'Historic Route 66 Corridor,'" explained Curtis. "there's been a modest boom in restoring old landmarks. But those projects are not simply nostalgia. The National Park Service is putting all this in a broader perspective. While some people following the highway found the American Dream, the opportunities at the end weren't available equally to all."

"Okay, okay," admitted Carol. "We get the point, guys. But, in the end you have to agree, we can't divide a fund drive into a dozen different parts."

That brought a new voice to the discussion: Tricia Bell came in from the hallway. Curtis recognized her immediately and, without thinking, called out, "Drum roll, please!"

"Thank you," smiled Tricia, taking a mock bow. "I apologize for showing up unannounced, but Jimmy told me about it. And since my group is planning a fundraiser here for Wounded Warriors, I decided to come for the weekend and poke my nose in your business."

Janet said, "We're an ad hoc group, so all classmates are welcome to contribute ideas . . . and money . . . to our 'business.'"

Curtis would later learn how Janet had set up Tricia's surprise appearance. And that, behind the scenes, Patrick had urged Eddie to be an active participant.

Jimmy explained, "Our good friend Gary organizes these

benefits all around the state, and Tricia's combo—'Cow-bell'—often performs. Most of you'll be gone home by then, but 'Cowbell' will be at The Table in two weekends."

"Well, that's convenient," Janet observed. "Tricia, we're involved in fundraising here, to cover the expenses of our grand celebration and to create a scholarship fund for a graduate who comes fifty years after us."

"Now," Sarah said, "we haven't quite agreed on the second part of that. Most of us think we . . . we need to take care of ourselves first. I mean, we've earned what we have and we deserve to enjoy ourselves a bit . . . you know, in our senior years."

"And" said John with a bit more anger in his voice "Too many people want to take it from us and give to others who haven't worked for it."

Curtis wanted to ask if those were the same people who taken our country from us.

"Gary told me some of this," admitted Tricia, "but I don't see it as an either/or situation. It can be neither, either/or, or both, as far as I'm concerned."

Betty was visibly upset. "You people who've had the lucky breaks in life may think we're all sitting on comfortable fortunes and can afford to chip in on anything you want to do. But for others—and I don't speak only for myself here—we have to budget our fixed incomes."

Curtis nodded sympathetically. "Patrick and I talked about this, and that's why we're saying we all make anonymous contributions, so there's no bragging or shaming. We're creating an account at Fairfield Central Bank, and you can use direct deposit or PayPal, cash or nothing. No one will post a scoreboard of donors and amounts."

Carol rose as if the conversation were over. "I say, we raise the money to fund the reunion first. And then, if some of you want to start a scholarship fund . . . And I think the only reasonable way to proceed is with one award. But . . . Sam and John and I were talking about this last night . . . we think such a drive would work best after the event, you know, around the Christmas season when everybody is in a giving mood."

Curtis knew that enthusiasm for any class project would drop off dramatically after the fall reunion. But he also sensed they had unintentionally given him an opening.

Tricia Bell also helped when she said: "I can provide a DJ for the event—a professional who won't cost us a dime."

All eyes were asking, so she smiled. "Why, me, of course! Plus Cowbell."

Chapter Twenty-six: Hearts

Out on Carol's patio, the official meeting over, Eddie returned to the question of who is responsible for America's growth and prosperity. "Nearly all of us contributed in some way, but I've also come to realize I'd missed a big chance to do more with wind power."

"How so?" asked Curtis. But he noted the twinkle in Eddie's eye, a clue that he might be going to embellish this tale.

Eddie went on. "I can explain, but first I need to acknowledge a physical restriction I didn't know I had until until my last birthday. That's when I learned that my inferior vena cava—the IVC—was on my left side, not the right as it is for more than 99.5% of all people. I had to tell my wife, 'Oh, my God. I'm left-hearted!'"

Curtis grinned. "I think a lot of us have known you're de-flictive."

"What are you talking about?" Tim asked, his beer poised short of his lips. "Your 'IVC'?"

Eddie explained. "All the blood in your lower trunk, abdomen, the pelvis and legs is carried by this—this giant tube—to the right atrium of the heart. An aortic aneurysm scan showed I had no aneurisms, but this major blood vessel is on the wrong damn side. And it means that my circuits are crossed. I was mis-wired before birth. Who knows what this has done?"

Sandra said, "Fifty years too late, you realized there was a road not taken."

"Right. If my stupid IVC had been on the right side, I'd be a wealthy man now, wealthy from windmills. I could have taken this acceptable, but ordinary reunion to a Branson level."

When they had all been in school, there was no "Las Vegas of the Midwest." The little town in the southwestern corner of the state was principally known as the home of the two-year School of the Ozarks. The mushrooming resort now hosts several million visitors annually.

Eddie explained that, after nearly twenty years as an Air Force systems engineer, building aircraft that took maximum advantage of air flow, he'd had a chance to switch to a start-up company making turbines for the latest hi-tech windmills.

A buddy approached him with "the chance of a lifetime." He and some friends had bought the rights to put windmills on a hundred miles of Wichita Mountain ridges in western Oklahoma. Their timing had been perfect as wind energy would boom in the early 21st century.

The group who launched the program had gone to what was in the 1960s South Central College of Missouri at Fairfield (formerly the School of Mines and Metallurgy), a fine science and technology school that, over the years gained university status and an even better reputation.

With a wistful look, Eddie recalled, "Twenty-five years ago I was still making the grades for promotion, looking at a generous fixed retirement plan. Much of what I did by then was to channel paperwork and people to the right places—smooth and easy is the flow."

"So, you lost touch with new developments," said Tim, a bit wistfully. "That happened to a lot of us."

Eddie nodded. "I have to admit, though, that this 'Molino Gigante' made my pulse flutter, a remarkable piece of workmanship. Strong but lightweight materials, it could withstand hurricane-strength winds. And its sealed, permanently lubricated parts would need almost no upkeep. Only a tornado landing right on top of one would do any damage."

"Most of us got stuck in ruts," Sandra observed philosophically. "You make it into your late 40s, early 50s, you get comfortable. It's hard to start over."

Eddie smiled. "So right! Standing out there on the isolated Oklahoma hilltop to survey my opportunity, I had a panic attack. It was not just about starting life all over again. I'd have to ask my family to leave the only home they'd known, find a new house, learn the neighborhoods in a different town, transfer money to other banks, switch church and civic memberships, hand over their bodies to new doctors. They'd done that as all military families do."

Sandra observed. "I've been out that way, near Fort Sill. There's something intimidating in the landscape—stark red rock, scrub trees battling prairie winds, hot summer baking the dirt, cold winters freezing the living."

"Yes. And, frankly, I've never been great at relocation. But I tell you, that company, that Molina Gigante Company took off. And, damn it, I could have retired a wealthy man at 55. If . . . ," he grinned dramatically, " . . . if I hadn't been left-hearted."

Gary said. "I should have that scan. I think I'm left-hearted, too."

"Uh-oh," said Tim. "Looks we need another round for another tall tale."

When everyone was settled again, Gary began. "I don't think any of you ever met Charlene Waters, a St. Louis girl. I took an interest in her because she was posting the highest scores in advanced mining engineering we were in together."

His wife Milly offered, "You also took an interest in her because she was good-looking." She met and married Gary after college and his time in the Army.

Gary grinned, squinting as if he saw Charlene now. "Hmm. Cascading blonde hair, crystal blue eyes, a slim, athletic body that slid into classrooms, seats, clothes. She was a bit hot." He saw Milly scowl. "Of course, I was mainly impressed with her mind."

Sandra nodded. "But, since we've all met your very beautiful wife of forty some years here, this Charlene must figure in some star-crossed lover story."

"Or a 'girl who got away' story," offered Tim,

"She turned out to be the girl who had already gotten away," Gary admitted. "But I didn't know that. So, young and foolish, I concocted a scheme to sweep her off her feet. I would show her the mine shaft two of my buddies had dug in a limestone cave."

Missouri is famous for its sinkholes, underground rivers, shut-ins, and caves. Most kids knew about them as places to play, to hide things, and to use for rendezvous.

"We all had to do an independent project for that course. And I told Charlene I knew where the two of us could install a one tenth scale mine elevator down into soft Missouri rock. 'We lower a grabbing mechanism,' I told her, 'like what you find in those bowling alley claw machines—and see what kind of rock or whatever we can bring up.'"

"You're pulling up a lump of something with a shovel right now," quipped Tim.

Gary ignored him. "Charlene agreed to go there after Friday's class. And when the day came, she glided among the hickory and oak, danced across creeks on rock stepping-stones, slipped into the hillside cave as if she'd made this trip a dozen times."

"You've become downright poetic there, fifty years after the fact," teased Milly. "But, as the rest of you will learn, Charlene wasn't all she seemed."

"Or maybe she was more," said Gary. "Anyway, I do remember how the flame of my kerosene lantern caught all her good features in that dark cave. I pointed out the eight-inch hole Bill, Jody, and I had bored through the floor by linking together sections of metal pipe, jamming an old boat propeller in the end, and cranking it with a car jack wrench until we broke through to an underground cavity."

"You didn't accidentally grab Charlene by the . . .?" asked Tim.

"Nah. I dropped a pebble into the opening to demonstrate

the vastness of what we named 'The Shaft.' " Groans from the group. "There were some splats, a plink, a finally a ker-plunk. 'Gold,' I told Charlene. 'Or oil or a tunnel to another Jesse James hideout.'"

They'd all visited nearby Meramec Caverns, the legendary outlaw's underground sanctuary, and been shown his secret exit route.

"Hey, it may be bull, but I thought it was working when she said, 'This is amazing. I'll build a wench system to send down some grappling jaws.' And I said I'd take pictures with my Polaroid. We'll get an A for sure."

"And you asked her to come to your room later to look at your . . . negatives."

"Don't I wish. But that's when she announced that she was another 'student's wife.' The words sucked the air from my lungs . . . and maybe the beauty out of the woods."

"Ah, it was the road already taken by someone else."

"And now, thanks to Eddie here, I realize it was not taken by me because . . . because I, too, suffer from undiscovered, unscanned, undiagnosed left-heartedness that sent me out in the woods at the wrong time."

Milly patted his hand. "It all turned out in the end: This sweet engineer poet took me to see his . . . uh, 'Shaft' a few years later."

Gary smiled. "And Charlene, truly a brilliant scientist, went through four husbands, a few bankrupt companies, and numerous lawsuits between then and now. Your destiny was sweeter."

He leaned over to give her a kiss.

Chapter Twenty-seven: Tears

After Curtis left the informal session at Carol's, he called Jackson, the bank president, on his cell phone, asking again about renting the house on Junction Street for the reunion weekend. He also wanted him to remind his younger brother about the reunion. While he'd mailed several announcements to Jackson, he wasn't sure he had passed them on or that Bill paid any attention to them.

He received some good news: the college student renters were willing to sublet for two evenings so that these eccentric seniors could relive their youth. Paperwork would be forthcoming from Jackson.

"I think the others are getting on board with this," Curtis told him. "I hope Bill has it on his calendar."

Jackson paused. "Well, it's on his calendar; I can say that. Whether he'll come or not is problematic. But I might guess there's a 75 per cent chance."

"I think the other two are coming, so that might tip the balance."

There was a pause. "Bill has gotten on a new kick lately. He claims he's found evidence that a Cherokee hideout in his cabin in the last century."

Curtis shrugged. "Certainly before our time. Why the interest?"

Another pause. "You might want to ask him yourself. He knows you're in town. Why not drive out there. I can let him know you're on the way."

Curtis realized he would have time, though he wondered

how Bill would already know about his being in town. Was Jackson tracking the reunion committee's work? Or were others in the group communicating with the class maverick? Still, he reasoned that a talk with Bill might encourage Susan to commit to bridge Déjà Vu.

He thanked Jackson and found the original directions he had given him tucked away in his folder with reunion year-book material. He decided he could go. Remembering his last visit, though, he took a white handkerchief with him.

As he wound up the narrow lane, he thought he saw something or someone moving in the trees beside the cabin. From what Jackson had told him and what he'd deduced from the bachelor state of the cabin, he was pretty sure Bill lived alone. The dense woods and his apprehension about what Bill might be up to probably inspired his imagination.

Still, he had his surrender flag ready and closed the car door noisily to announce his arrival. Bill come out onto the porch smiling.

"Curtis, you sly devil. Jack told me you might come out."

"Hey, good buddy. I just thought I should remind you of the big get-together—not so many months away."

"I do have it on my calendar, but come on up, have a seat, and make your pitch."

Curtis took a wooden rocker on the porch, and, thinking it would be good to ease into the conversation, said, "So, Jackson says you're . . . um . . . researching the history of this place." He gestured at the log wall behind him, which, he guessed, could be over a hundred years old. He heard some rustling in the bushes beside him.

Bill's eyes light up. "Yes, yes—history. You know about

the Trail of Tears, I'm sure."

"Thousands of Cherokees—men, women, and children—driven from their homes in the Southeast to places in Oklahoma. Something like 100,000, as I recall."

"Right. Off lands white people wanted. They were force-marched to lands no one wanted. The irony being, of course, that years later oil would make those Native Americans wealthy. Well, the few descendants of those who survived."

"Right. Disease, exhaustion, starvation. President Jackson's 'Indian Removal' program was anything but humane. So, you think one of the Cherokee nation settled here?"

Bill grinned. "I have evidence of it. Her descendant comes to me many nights."

"Uh-oh," thought Curtis. Out loud, he asked, "I . . . I didn't see any other homes in the drive up. Where does . . . your friend live?"

"Oh, it's not far away. If . . . if you want to stay until it gets dark, when Yona usually comes, you can talk to her, too."

"Um, I've got a Skype call set up with Susan Howe this evening—you know, to confirm her travel plans for the fall, the bridge game and all." Curtis was happy to have a genuine excuse not to stay.

"She's not dangerous, if that's your worry," said Bill. "She just likes to tell what happened to her ancestors. One of the routes of the Trail of Tears came through Fairfield."

"I think I read about that possibility. The main groups went south of here, I thought, along what is now Route 60."

"True, but Amadahy was with a few families that came this way. They were then marched down to Springfield, connecting to the main caravan. That was almost 100 years before Route 66, the more famous trail, was established. It was, they say, the 'Mother Road,' but the mothers like Amadahy didn't become famous representations of the American Dream. Quite the opposite."

Curtis knew wooden "Indians" were still positioned in front of roadside stores. And many of the knickknack memorabilia tourists bought perpetuated the stereotype of "savage redskin."

Again, he heard sounds in the woods off the porch, less a rustling of leaves or branches and more the whispering of wind or murmuring of water. "You're right about this tragic part of our history," he admitted to Bill. "But Amadahy, did you say? Did she survive the journey?"

"Only in a manner of speaking," said Bill in a way that made Curtis raise his eyebrows.

"Her daughter survived. You see, Amadahy was carrying an infant child who, as they moved across the Mississippi River, became sick. She wouldn't eat, became lethargic, was most certainly dying. The soldiers leading the Cherokee did not stop or provide aid, of course, so Amadahy, keeping her baby wrapped in bits of blanket, fell behind."

"Are you going to tell me she and her baby found a home in or close to Fairfield."

"I am," said Bill with a stern look. "You see, Amadahy had fed her daughter herbs that made her appear sick. It was her escape plan. She found this very cabin unoccupied. In fact, Yona is her eighth generation descendent. She's pure blood Cherokee and technically owns this land." He waved an arm at the woods around them.

Curtis thought native Americans rejected the white man's

idea of "ownership," but decided not to suggest it. "So, so, some men settled here, too? I can't say I remember a . . . um . . . community of Native Americans in the country."

"That's another interesting part of the story: each daughter in the line from Amadahy to Yona has made the trek out to western Oklahoma to find a husband. They go by foot, never traveling on roads . . . roads like Route 66."

"And there's a gathering of eligible bachelors for her to choose from out there?"

Bill sighed. "Yes, I guess to people like you, who accept conventional histories, this sounds fantastic. Locals have no objections to the resurrection of Route 66, with the renovated motels and gas stations. And they're proud of the 'Historic Route 66' signs on Interstate 44 access roads and town streets; but they hide as well as highlight the past."

Curtis felt he needed to agree if he was going to get Bill to join the bridge game. "Well, you're right that there are aspects of this nostalgic movement that trouble me. Much of the highway's golden years were times of hidden divisions in our society, of a blindness to those left out of the American Dream."

Bill seemed pleased to hear this, "So, Curtis, perhaps the Cherokee nation, invisible for a long time, is reappearing, too. A people who've been living off the grid, in the spaces between the lines, are taking shape, it might seem, out of thin air."

"Wasn't this area inhabited by the Osage?"

"Mostly, yes. But the Northern Cherokee Nation is seeking to be federally recognized as Native American tribe. And Yona is the leader of these people."

Curtis peered into the woods. "That makes . . . sense, I guess. But where do you fit in, Bill. Are you working, behind the scenes, as it were, to help Yona?"

Bill stood up. "I'd better not say too much, Curtis. As they say, what you don't know . . . Well, I think it's time for you to go now."

Curtis was not unhappy to be on his way. "I do have to get back into town to Skype with Susan. Can I tell her you likely to be a fourth in the fall?"

Bill opened the door and crossed the threshold but turned to say, "I have a feeling it's going to be an . . . an interesting event for the town of Fairfield. So, yes, tell her I'll be there."

Chapter Twenty-eight: Gaps

"So," he later told Susan in his Skype call, "it's all a go. I'm assuming, of course that you're in now."

Despite his optimistic tone, Curtis' confidence that there would Bridge Game Déjà Vu had dropped considerably as he drove back to town. He had to wonder if Bill would be a suitable participant in any group project.

Susan laughed. "You're pinning the success or failure of this on me, aren't you? You know, I chatted with Cindy not long ago, and she admitted she still has doubts."

But he insisted, "Oh, that hook has been set. She's coming."

"Didn't she need you to do something for her to be sure she would come? Finding some town records she wanted?"

"I've filled out the paperwork. However, as you might expect, it's going to take at least a few weeks for them to locate and copy them." Actually, Curtis had not been assured by the tone of the town officials, understandably suspicious about this unusual request. Again, he felt he could be taking two steps back after one forward.

"Well," concluded Susan, "let me put myself in the same category as Cindy: I probably will be able to come. Did you find out about the Castle house?"

"I've got all the paperwork for the sublet agreement." Now he had to decide whether to make it final or not. The down payment was the full amount.

"How about this," offered Susan. "I'll be in Norfolk in a couple of weeks. I could come down to your North Carolina place for half a day. I'll make sure I could clear my schedule for the reunion between now and then. I do have one concern I'd rather discuss in person than over the phone."

She said this with a curious earnestness, so Curtis had to accept her proposal. He asked, though, what new hidden issue would be revealed by Susan, possibly forcing more revision of his plans?

Before he called it a night he reviewed a message from Barbara Lemon: classmates still in town tomorrow afternoon could meet for a last indulgence at Maid Rite. And she had the latest contact information she wanted to pass on for him to include in the yearbook.

Given what he'd learned on this trip, he was preparing to use his editorial prerogative to frame the class story in a more inclusive (some would say revisionist) frame. To that end, he checked out of the motel early in order to attend the service at Liberation Baptist Church.

The building was full, and the ushers had to bring out extra folding chairs in the back. He noted that there were several white families present and some individuals who seemed to him possibly Asian or Mediterranean.

Curtis had been to weddings, funerals, and commemorative services in African-American churches in Rural, so, despite his own membership in a traditional—if not conservative—Episcopalian congregation, he was comfortable in the call-and-response nature of the sermon, the hymns in which the congregation was as loud as the choir, the mounting intensity of the sermon that brought many forward in the concluding alter call.

While he felt Abraham was seeking him out as they sang more more verses of "Just as I Am," he kept his gaze up, as if contemplating an assured place in heaven rather than needing to make a statement of faith on earth. Since his father, a scientist, was not a churchgoer, Curtis had learned early to resist dividing people into the saved and the damned.

After the service the pastor was waiting at the door to shake hands and greet visitors, and Curtis complimented on the sermon. "I'm not sure I've heard that particular passage preached on, so your words were new to me. I will have to think about what you said."

Abraham's text came from Zechariah: "Do not be like your fathers, to whom the former prophets proclaimed, saying, 'Thus says the LORD of hosts, "Return now from your evil ways and from your evil deeds "'" But they did not listen or give heed to Me," declares the LORD."

His new friend smiled and said, "Carry them in your heart."

At the assisted care facility/nursing home they met Jefferson Brown. He was a man in his nineties who had spent years researching the African American presence in Fairfield and the surrounding counties.

"I'm sure Abraham has told you," Curtis said, "that I could use some help filling in the history of Fairfield. After the Civil War, for instance, did former slaves settle here?"

"Blacks, free and slave, have lived in the region as long as whites," smiled the World War Two veteran and retired mechanic. "After the Civil War, Missouri drafted a new constitution that required public education be made available to blacks. We, in fact, made up nearly one quarter of Fairfield's citizens at the time."

Curtis nodded. "Of course, the total population would have been small then, but that's certainly more than I would have thought. Something must have attracted them here."

"Education could have been one thing. To find teachers for the new black school (the old white school remained, of course, segregated), they offered salaries better than those paid to female white teachers. And in 1882 they completed a new school building, the church building where Brother Abraham is the shepherd now."

Curtis thought a minute. "You know, we had a centennial celebration when I was, oh, about ten years old, I guess. And I can't recall a single reference to blacks in town history."

Jefferson observed, "That would have been in the '50s. After the war, whites thought the black soldiers ought to be satisfied to return to the status they'd left. But they'd seen a bit of the world and were demanding change."

"Ah, Little Rock in '57, for instance. Back in Virginia there were protests, too."

"The Great Migration of the 20s and 30s—black families leaving the old plantation states of the South for economic opportunities in the Midwest and North—brought a lot of us to the big cities, St. Louis and Kansas City. But when some found no jobs, say, in St. Louis, they continued—down that new highway Route 66—to this area. We wanted more for our children."

"Since there were jobs, many fit right in," explained Abraham. "Of course, there were times when they could see in some people's eyes that they were viewed as not just another race, but almost another species. That attitude seldom emerged in public, though."

"I don't remember any of that, but I'm afraid I wasn't conditioned to see it. For that reason, I'm interested in informing my classmates who were similarly not fully aware of your history. It would be best if I could do it in such a way that it would illuminate our current situation in the nation. It's not as if the entire population has accepted a black President."

"You're about the age of Sonja Brown, aren't you?" the octogenarian asked. "Now, she she's had quite a distinguished career. Her story might help."

"I'm embarrassed to say I don't remember her from high school; but I have asked if she could expand the very short biographical note she submitted for the yearbook."

"Get her to talk about her career as one of the first graduates of the university school of architecture. And her two tours with the Peace Corps. And her stint with the State Department. She's received a number of honorary degrees."

"I certainly will! How is that I didn't—don't—know any of this?"

He chuckled. "To see how she became invisible, you might go back to her acceptance at the Summer Program for Outstanding High School Students at the University of Missouri."

"I remember that program: my sister went. She was . . . is .

. . a math genius. As I recall, it was two weeks with other students selected from different counties around the state. There are over one hundred counties, but only about twenty-five nominated a student."

"That's right. So, it was quite a prize to be chosen as the one representative from Fairfield High School, a very good system. But the town paper didn't include her picture with the story."

"What? That must have been an oversight." Curtis saw the eyebrows of both Abraham and Jefferson go up. "Or maybe not."

"Listen, young man," said the resident. "You find out what you can. When you have questions, you write me care of this other young man." He slapped Abraham on the shoulder.

It was his own fault, of course, that Curtis knew nothing of newspaper bias, never having questioned a culture that made people of color invisible. But he also saw that this was not just an individual shortcoming. If the local news organizations were biased in their reporting, it was also a public perspective that had been selective. How could he now address this issue in the yearbook in a way that would enlighten but not offend?

Chapter Twenty-nine: Substitutions

At the Maid Rite, Curtis got the address list from Barbara and also had a chance to talk with Tricia. He said his mother had reminded him that's she'd been a Miss Route 66 contestant.

"Ah," she said. "The true story of that event has only been

told in recent years."

"Could you enlighten me?" asked Curtis. "I'm curious. And all the stories I've been hearing are preparing me to put together a great reunion yearbook."

She smiled. "This shouldn't really go in there, but I can tell you. It begins at Fanny's Dairy Delite, where I worked, not at school. You see, Mr. Pierce, assistant high school principal and long-time promoter of the pageant, dropped by one afternoon when I was working to order a vanilla shake. He said he had a few tips that might help me in the upcoming competition."

"A bit irregular, but at least in a public place."

"It was a slow time. So, I joined him in a booth on my break. He did something rather unexpected . . . at least by the young me. He dipped his index finger—cigarette-browned, by the way—into a glass of water. 'If, Tricia,' he said, 'I put my wet finger on the lip of the glass. . . . . '"

Curtis raised his eyebrows. "Hmm. I know this trick."

"All the older girls had told me I should . . . play up to him . . . whenever possible. So, I watched him innocently. He said, 'If I circle a glass of water,' his finger moving slowly around the rim. '. . . with just the right pressure, at just the right speed--like this--it will make a note.'"

Curtis said. "Yes. A sound will come, a ringing hollow tone."

"I associated it with the wind's moaning on a winter night in some romantic castle: 'Ooooo,' sang the glass. Mr. Pierce's lips make a round shape that would produce that Ooooo."

"We hear the sound differently, of course, in our current era," admitted Curtis.

"Simple me back then! I just said, 'That's neat!' and took the straw out of my glass so I could try the same thing on my side of the booth. I was putting it on a paper napkin when Mr. Pierce reached across the booth and stopped my hand. His fingers wrapped gently around my wrist, he leaned forward and looked me directly in the eyes. I noticed an oddly excited look in his eyes and extra spit gathering at one corner of his mouth."

Curtis realized that, although this had happened more than fifty years ago, Tricia was remembering it in sharp detail. Post-traumatic stress was not only a reaction to men's experience in war, but also too often a consequence of men using power to seduce women. He also knew victims sometimes get release by telling the story to others.

Tricia went on. "Then he said, 'I can put my finger on another place.' His voice had gone down to husky whisper. 'If I do, you'll make the same sound: 'Ooooo.' He leaned closer. 'You'll do a belly dance. 'Ooooo.' His voice dropped to a whisper. 'And love it. Ooooo.'"

Curtis rose up out of his seat. "You must have been ready to jump out of our skin."

"I was. In fact, I jumped up and ran out of the store, terrified. I didn't understand exactly what he was talking about, but all my instincts screamed, 'Get out of here now!'"

Curtis mused. "But it seems like the experience has stayed with you all this time."

She shrugged. "Yes. I worked through it a few years ago. That's when I realized he and I could never have . . . made music together."

Curtis raised his eyebrows.

"You see, I have a deep belief in an underlying order in this universe. It's so old with me I've concluded it must have grown out of my childhood—well, our childhood. As you know, we both grew up in a close neighborhood, several dozen parents raising a generation of young people in an area so unified everyone called it the Circle.'"

"Yes!" Curtis agreed enthusiastically. "The loop made by its three principal streets--Oak, Hill, and Limestone--gave us the sense that we were living within a ring of magic."

"That new section on the edge of town was magic. Frame and brick two-bedroom homes built to keep pace with growth during World War II and in the boom years afterward. Even into our teenage years, our world remained connected, contained within supportive boundaries. Our high school cruising route even completed a circle: Main Street out to Business Route 66 (also called Kingshighway) past Fanny's Dairy Delite around to Sixth Street, back up to Main. We'd make that circuit ten times in the course of a Friday or Saturday night, seeing the same sights but refreshing ourselves with every trip."

Curtis seldom took that same route, more often on weekends headed over to Bill Castle's house for an evening of bridge. But that, too, had its symbolic structure: the square card table, the four players, the orderly dealing and playing.

She continued. "My family was also a harmonious whole as father, mother, older sister, and I shared a sense of destiny, the wholeness of clan. Not that we thought of ourselves as upper class, but we were the Bells of Fairfield, Missouri, nuclear family in a small town at the heart of the country. Even the onomatopoetic sound of my name--my maiden name, that is, 'Bell'--asserts, to me at least, the resonance of a perfect note, intention and fulfillment in one sound."

Curtis smiled in agreement, though there was a certain envy of her confidence in this order of the universe. Too many later events had shaken his beliefs. And his own nuclear family had been based more on exclusion than inclusion. Eventually, outside forces had intruded on that unit.

"Life was a lovely song for me until twelfth grade," Tricia insisted, "until I got caught up in the Route 66 Pageant. And something, or someone, broke the spell, ended the age of innocence. Mr. Pierce, yes. But there were also others who came later."

Curtis nodded again. "But you said you learned that his proposal was . . . without force? And that your faith was restored somehow?"

"Yes. You see, I didn't understand his intentions then, of course, for at least two reasons: I hadn't yet realized my own power; and I didn't understand his lack of it."

Curtis raised his eyebrows again, wanting an explanation.

She sighed. "I hope my chief source of strength is immaterial, my heart and my character. My family and friends say it's so. But I also know a significant portion of what force I can exert in a man's world comes from my body, more specifically my belly."

Curtis knew it was so. She had a beautiful face, but she also had a beautiful body. He hadn't had the tools as an adolescent to identify and analyze the desire a boy feels for a girl. She has "a good figure," or "an hour-glass body," or "legs that go all the way up?" What do these terms mean? And why are boys' eyes drawn to features of one body and not another?

When he recalled this girl from the other side of the Circle—in the dresses required at school and the neighborhood play clothes—her hips and breasts were united by a slender waist.

As if reading his mind (and the minds of all the boys and men she'd known), Tricia said "I have always had an unusually small, flat stomach. My breasts were modest, my rear end appealing enough. But the way my hips are hung, my flat tummy--even after three children--moves, rocks, swivels, and bumps in ways that, it turns out, men can't seem to resist."

Curtis had always wondered how closely women studied their own bodies, in full-length mirrors at home and in the triple mirrors of department stores. But he was taken aback by Tricia's straightforward (and accurate) self-assessment.

"Well," she went on, "this was something I was just beginning to learn when Mr. Pierce made his indecent proposal. It came as our generation learned first the Twist and then other pelvis-oriented dances. And all this at the time fashion was lowering the line where we wore our jeans and tightening the tops of our skirts. I could do, you see, a belly dance."

"Tricia Bell with her alluring middle was an unconsciously seductive object of desire?"

"She was. I also know now why the same man made so much of his finger and the note it could sound on a glass of water. Even my sweet husband of forty-five years has acknowledged that a middle-aged man cannot always, shall we say, rise to the occasion. And I'm pretty sure that Route 66 Pageant official was confessing that leverage was, for him, a recurring problem."

Curtis tried to show no change in his expression but felt a wince.

Tricia looked at him, and when he said nothing, she went on. "I had no idea at that time about substitutions in the game of love. There were, so far as I knew, one male organ, one female organ, and one position for those involved. What a range of options, equipment, partners, goals my own daughters knew about in their teenage years!"

This time Curtis could smile in agreement. "So, Mr. Pierce's proposal, on the other hand (so to speak), was not for what he could actually have. Ooooo!"

They joined in a loud but slightly uneasy laugh together.

Chapter Thirty: Status

When Susan drove down from Norfolk to their river house later that year, Curtis assumed he'd be introducing Beth to a complete stranger, a woman who'd grown up in the Midwest and then spent most of her life in California. When he explained that his high school classmate, Susan Howe, would be down for a very brief visit, her response was a surprise.

"Susan Howe? The founder of Woman's Body Susan Howe? You're telling me that she grew up in Fairfield?"

"Well, yes. She was one of the bridge players. How do you know about her?"

"She's famous. I've read two of her books about women's health. Wait here."

Beth went out to the bookcases he'd constructed in their living room and came back quickly with *Antibody: A Guide to Medical His-story*.

"She's one of the revolutionary doctors who began advocating health care that recognizes female issues as different from male issues. You know, a basic fairness dictates that we spend less money on treating erectile dysfunction and more on managing menopause."

"Ah, yes, well . . . ." Curtis was thinking how he could pretend that he, of course, knew how important Susan was and therefore had specially orchestrated this visit.

Beth interrupted his thoughts. "If she's going to be here tomorrow, we'd better clean up a bit. She may be the most important person to ever come to Hartford! I'll make that new minestrone soup you like for lunch, and you plan on your wonderful sour cream biscuits."

Curtis had listened for years to Beth talk with her women friends about feminist books and authors, though he knew he tuned out a lot of details. In his own field, he had adopted new critical methodologies and included "rediscovered" women authors in his courses. But he suspected he wouldn't get away with a lie that he'd brought Susan here to please her.

But the two women were instant friends, and Curtis was almost excluded from the lunch conversation. They were eating in the family room, which had an expansive river view.

"What nice things you have!" Susan said, turning the plate over to inspect it.

"Those are Wedgwood, passed down from my great-grandmother. Curtis and I married during graduate school and took some time to get professionally established, so we would never have bought this kind of china. In fact," she waved at the cabinet on the other side of the room, "almost everything we have was given to us by parents and grandparents."

Curtis agreed. "Much of the furniture you see, the paintings on the walls, the pillows in the chairs are all from family. None of it is especially valuable, except to us because they remind us of those who cared for us."

"I envy you that," said Susan with what Curtis thought was a sad tone.

When Beth later began to clear the table, Susan apologized for being about to monopolize Curtis. "We're not up to anything secretive," she laughed. "It's just reunion business, so, listen in and join in whenever you want. I'm explaining to your husband how the gathering might be an opportunity I hadn't anticipated."

Beth smiled. "Beyond a few rubbers of bridge with some eccentric seniors?"

They all laughed. Then Susan began her discussion of the "concern" she had not wanted to discuss on the phone. "Did you know, Curtis, that I was adopted?"

"Uh, no, I guess not. But I suppose it's not something I would have asked anyone about back then. And I don't know if it's something someone would announce, not that there's any stigma to it that I'm aware of."

Susan shook her head. "It was a problem for me, maybe not for all adoptees. I'm not sure I was embarrassed, exactly, when I first learned, though it came as enough of a surprise that I kept it to myself for . . . for some years."

"I can see how a young person might think her birth parents had abandoned him or her. But someone could also be an orphan, in fact, a relative of the adopting parents."

"Yes. But as you may know, most adoptions back then were kept secret. Neither the child nor the new parents knew anything of the baby's past. That was the case for me, though, much, much later I learned the truth."

Curtis thought for a moment. "You're making me realize—or confirm—that I grew up with a default picture of all of us: two parents, the father worked, the mother stayed home. I knew of no divorced parents, no young widows or widowers, no absent 'birth parents.'"

She smiled. "I believe that's why I didn't know that I was adopted until I was turning sixteen. And I found out more by accident than any decision by my . . . by the parents I knew."

"I'm sorry that I can't call up a picture of them. Well, I'm not sure I have mental images of any parents except those of my close friends and the few girls I dated."

She nodded. "It turns out I resembled my adoptive parents physically, at least enough that no one questioned if we were related. We're short, dark haired, a bit square-faced. And I had no siblings that you would compare me with."

"Again, that seems consistent with the way we saw things back then. Just like the houses so many of us grew up in—regular two-bedroom with attached garage on a small lot—everyone fit in one or two categories. The houses were brick or wood, bedrooms on the side or along the back, sidewalk from the street or off the driveway. So, we were only child, had one sibling or possibly two, there may or may not have been a live-in grandparent. Everyone belonged in one of a very few boxes."

"I certainly understood myself in that way. The only slightly odd thing was the age of my parents. Most of their friends, parents of my friends, were born around 1920; but mine were a dozen years older. That might have been a clue for me, if I'd know more as a child."

"Now that you mention it: couples had their children in

their twenties. Whether that was because there was less—and less effective—birth control or that it was simply expected. So, your parents weren't able to have children on their own?"

"That's right. They married some years before the war, and my dad served in the Pacific—Hawaii, Guam, the Philippines. He came home with an infant girl—me."

"Your mom was in Fairfield?"

"No, she was in Belleville, Illinois, outside St. Louis. Father was with the 8th Army before and after the war. His last post was Leonard Wood, and I went to junior high school in Waynesville. Then we moved to Fairfield. Mother wanted to live where there was a college, and Father was being courted to work with the Geological Survey after he got out of the Army."

"I see. I'm not sure, though, I understand why you had to tell me all this in person. It's not, um, shocking. And I suspect there are other adoption cases that we weren't aware of."

"Yes." Susan paused, taking a deeper breath. "But you might notice now that I'm bit more dark-skinned than, say, either of you."

"Okay. Again, a physical feature that doesn't reveal much, as far as I'm concerned."

"No, not so much now. Still, in high school my mother was careful to make me use facial make-up to . . . lighten my complexion. She had some special creams that made me resemble . . . well, everyone else."

Curtis asked. "Are you saying there's a racial issue here?"
"My biological mother was an Army nurse in Manilla, the Philippines. When the Japanese invaded in 1942, many from her unit fled; others were taken prisoner. But she was taken in

by . . . by a native family. The father of the family was my father."

"Ah."

"Their brief affair was, I believe, consensual. He was a doctor, and they'd worked together. I only found out by accident one day. Looking for a paperclip in my father's desk, I came across this faded envelope of old paper, thin oilskin documents. They were copies of my adoption papers he'd had to produce to write a will. They included a 1944 death certificate for my mother. It turns out my legal identity was . . . um, complicated. As was, in fact, my parentage, my citizenship, my race."

Beth, who'd listened carefully to Susan's account, said, "Given some of the talk we're hearing about this country and who belongs here, there are some truths about our past involvement in other countries that need to be acknowledged. To be honest on this, especially regarding countries we've been to war in, this will be a difficult process."

It would turn out Susan was more than capable of taking on this task.

Book Four: All
Chapter Thirty-one: Courts

After relaying what had happened at the final reunion planning meeting, Curtis was pleased to find his mother agreeing that, in her 100th year, she would attend. He had learned from Carol that all his talk about the past had made her a bit wistful at times. Over the phone she told her brother, "She even admitted to me recently that she been thinking more about the children she'd lost and could never recover."

"That's sad," he admitted. "But where she is on her journey, not necessarily a terrible thing."

Carol agreed. "We forget we Mom had a baby sister for one year when she was four. She died—one of those infant diseases. And she suffered a miscarriage before Louis was born. She said to me something like, 'I believe in my heart we will all—Oscar, too, of course—be gathered together soon. And I know that the emptiness that comes over me rarely— but now and then—will finally be filled.'"

Talking to his mother back in North Carolina, Curtis said, "You know, when I told classmates that you hope to be there, they were very enthusiastic."

"I doubt if many of them ever really knew me, as generally unsocial as our family was. They're probably curious to see what the last of our generation is like in her very old age."

"Not true, Mom. Tricia Bell, in fact, asked about you before she even knew you were still with us. She lived in our neighborhood, as you remember, so may have been one of the masked trick-or-treaters at your door. And Susan Howe, now a doctor, recalled that you used to volunteer at the hospital. Who knows which of my friends' fingers you stuck to check blood type?"

"Well, I think I'll enjoy seeing some of the class, but I'm also going for my own reasons. I want to drive by our old house, visit any of the old shops downtown still there in the age of Walmart, viewing changes at the university where your father taught. I'll be doing what the rest of you are—taking an indulgent, nostalgic look at yesteryear."

There was a twinkle in her eye as she said this, and Curtis wondered if she had other specific goals for the trip. As sturdy as she'd been her whole life, he couldn't dismiss the idea that she was making some unknown plans for her future.

Beth had researched ways for Mid to travel comfortably to St. Louis, where she'd rest up for a few days at the house of his brother Louis and wife Suzanne. Then it was just a two-hour drive down to Fairfield and the three-day weekend. Carol and husband Mark had volunteered to escort her to events whenever Curtis had specific reunion duties and to be with her and Beth during the now-famous Castle Bridge Déjà Vu.

Carol teased Curtis in the phone call from her home in California. "I may have to stop by the game to see my one-time almost date, Bill Castle. From what you tell me he's fulfilled his potential for weirdness."

"That and then some," agreed Curtis. "In fact, I'm a bit nervous about what he might do—not so much at the game but during the reunion's big event Saturday night."

"I suspect he'll talk a lot of guff but retreat into his shell when festivities begin."

"Does this prediction derive from your, um, exchanges with him back in high school?" teased Curtis.

"Don't go there, brother," she responded. He knew that

tone and kept quiet.

The card players were to meet at the old Castle house on the Friday afternoon of the reunion weekend to play a few rubbers. Then those that chose to would go to the opening social hour, but all would return for a second round of cards later in the evening.

Or at least that was the plan Curtis had outlined and to which no one had openly objected. Whether it would materialize as he imagined was to be seen. As a bit of insurance, he began sending them email updates that he hoped would increase their desire to see each other and to share stories of how they'd come from there to here, from long ago point A to present point B.

After Susan's visit, Curtis had realized how many individual tales he'd heard that complicated the group's story: "old soldier" Gary's in-country R & R in Vung Tau; Sandra's blood donor whose "bubba bubba bubba bubba" called up a tragic infant's death; Betty's senior year pregnancy; the downward spiral of Betty's friend Bob ending in a fatal car crash; Cindy's mother as victim of "McCarthyism"; Eddie's "left-hearted" destiny; Gary's walk in the woods with Charlene Waters; Tricia's teenage encounter with a would-be sexual predator; Bill's contrast of the Trail of Tears with the mythology of Route 66; Susan's revelation of her biological mother's life and early death.

He was determined to acknowledge the trials as well as the triumphs in the reunion yearbook. He decided a prologue by the editor would include parts of many of these stories, each would be attributed to "a classmate." If he did it right, no one would immediately identify the subject. Including these references had proven as difficult as any academic writing he'd ever done! More than once he had to scrap a draft and begin it all over again in a different way.

He considered his own children's growing up in Rural, Virginia. They, too, might not have recognized some of the less positive elements of their world. He recalled the junior sports league that was just getting established when his older son was in school. He and his siblings were excited about the new opportunity but didn't understand the historical reasons it was the first racially mixed youth program in the town.

Down Home Youth Sports was ad hoc at best, and, with no facilities, they had to make use of old school playgrounds, under-used parks, farm pastures of sympathetic supporters. Curtis saw both progress and regression in the process.

Justin, for instance, played basketball in the National Guard armory, and its shortcomings had been painful to the parents. (The kids, of course, just wanted to play.) The building had been used for the white school that appeared when, to resist integration, the town closed the public schools. So, Curtis and Beth felt ghosts of "the lost generation" flitting among the children.

It was a winter sport, and the Armory's heat was irregular. There were no bleachers, and the concrete floor was cold. Families brought folding chairs and wore their winter coats. But the worst feature was the defective time clock, borrowed from who knew where.

The boys played two fifteen-minute halves. A third of them were too small or too young to throw the basketball as high as the goal. A handful could dribble. So, a final score of 10 to 8 was not the result of a deliberate slow-down strategy.

Near the end of a game the parents and siblings would be pacing and shivering on the sidelines. They watched the clock and prayed for the referee to announce the end. But the clock would mysteriously short-circuit before it reached 00:00. There would be two minutes left, then 90 seconds, then—inexplicably—the clock would revert to two minutes, and a new count-down would begin. Two steps forward, two steps back.

The kids played on quite happily, calling for the ball, insisting they were fouled, bunching up around the one player who, if close to the basket, had the strength to score. The clock ran down again to a few seconds, then added minutes to the game. It was as bad as Groundhog's Day would be for Bill Murray in the movie of that name a decade later.

Now it seemed that Curtis would work for several hours to refine a section of *Confluence II*, convinced the total time necessary for yearbook work had been shortened significantly. But with each new communication, or some memory called up from the past, or a sudden inspiration for better presentation, he would turn the clock back, leave the 21st century and end up in high school rethinking what it all meant. A follow-up letter from Tricia Bell, for instance, had brought up another of his children's youthful sports events.

Tricia reminded him that in Fairfield there had been no extracurricular sports except little league baseball. And that was boys only. But she and half a dozen kids in the neighborhood decided one summer day to construct their own basketball court. Some discarded fence pickets were confiscated and hammered together to make a backboard. An empty lot across the street from the Lindstrom home was deemed an appropriate site.

Then they found a fallen tree trunk, hacked off the little side branches, and bolted their backboard to one end. They pooled allowance money to purchase the only manufactured part of their court: a hoop with white cord net, which they bolted to the backboard. Then they lowered the trunk into a hole they'd dug in the clay, tamping some large rocks around the base, and raked debris away from an area in front to create the court.

It was dirt, to be sure, though the hours of dribbling and setting picks and pushing for rebounds over time packed it down firmly. They played in all kinds of weather, shooting with gloves on and shuffling in galoshes. There was a streetlight across the road, so they would be out well into the evening. From his bedroom Curtis could hear the older kids laughing, celebrating, claiming victory. Echoes of that innocent time seemed to arise out of the pages of the reunion yearbook he was assembling.

Tricia had sent a grainy black and white photo of the site. In the shadows behind the self-made basketball court Curtis saw something moving. It was a memory of an encounter he realized he'd suppressed for more than sixty years. Now it was emerging into the light, and he did not want to see it.

Chapter Thirty-two: Clubs

Before he saw clearly what had been highlighted from the past by Tricia's letter and photo, Curtis received a call from Tim Carlson. He wanted Curtis to be more comfortable with the idea of a veterans' recognition moment at the reunion.

Curtis admitted, "I want to make sure all of us are recognized for what we did for our country—the teachers, doctors and nurses, government workers. But . . . "

Tim anticipated. "You're worried we'll stir up old hostilities? Anti-war vs. warrior?"

"Something like that. Again, we all want a good time, and to me that means not fighting old battles all over again."

"I understand; but let me tell a little story that may change your mind. I've given versions of it to civic organizations over the last few years."

"I have time to listen."

"This is about a prehistoric hunter/gatherer living in a cave along a hillside, right . . . right where Fairfield would be built thousands of years in the future."

Curtis smiled and said, "I'm not sure there were humans in our area that far back, but I'll allow the anachronism."

"I appreciate it. Now, Dan has mouths to feed--a wife and children. They're all hungry. But of late he's only been able to catch a slow, skinny rabbit, roast an occasional scrawny squirrel on a spit. And the hungrier he feels, the less strong he becomes. He needs food."

Curtis clucked his tongue in feigned sympathy. "Um-um."

Tim goes on. "There is, Dan knows, a wild boar living farther up the valley. He's seen him grazing in a clearing along a stream. But the animal is huge, too much for him to take on, too strong for any trap he can build. But, oh, what a supply of meat that boar would provide for Dan, Sally, and the kids if cooked in a pot over a slow fire with the right roots and herbs!"

"He needs a friend!"

"Exactly. And he thinks to himself, 'There's that other guy . . . there's Billy, who lives on the other hill, across the creek. Together we could kill that old pig and share the bacon."

Curtis agrees, "A man, a Dan, a plan!"

Jimmy chuckles. "Dan explains his plan to Billy, who's just as thin and hungry as he is. Billy will flush the boar from the other side of the clearing down to where the creek winds between two large rocks, a narrow passageway. And when there's no room to turn, Dan will hop out in front of him and ram his spear into the boar's chest. From behind Billy, will jump on the impaled pig and hack away with his stone knife. They'll kill that boar."

Curtis raised a hand. "Nowadays, Jimmy, stories have got to have blood and sex. You've got violence; is sex coming in our story?"

"You bet. But first, there has to be . . . there has to be crime and punishment." He pauses dramatically. "The boar drives Dan back, and Billy's first thrusts with his dagger are ineffectual. But they renew their attack, hacking and stabbing, and--it is a mess! After a ferocious struggle, they find themselves on opposite sides of their kill, kneeling and gasping from the effort."

Tim gasps on the phone, and Curtis is tempted to gasp in response.

"Dan, panting, looks across the body of their prey at Billy, also panting and thinks to himself" 'You know, if I didn't have Billy, I could keep this whole thing for myself. Well, and for my family. We'd get our strength back and . . . shoot, we could take a little to Billy's family.'"

"Uh-oh," said Curtis warily.

"So, suddenly, Dan jumps over the dead boar, grabs Billy by the neck, pushes him over on his back, bangs his head against some rocks, squeezes his windpipe until blood erupts from his nostrils . . . Billy's dead!"

Tim switches to a solemn voice. "Just then, some sort of judge comes along. We can call her 'God,' I suppose. And God says, 'There's a dead man here. Who's responsible for this wrong?' Dan can say, 'not me,' but there's blood on his hands, isn't there, literally and figuratively? God knows who killed Billy. And that's when the lightning bolt comes down, and all that's left of Dan is a greasy spot on the grass beside the dead boar. Phroomp!"

Curtis admits, "You have my attention. But what's the moral here, how does it explain the recognition of veterans at the reunion?"

"Stay with me now. I just need to add a slight twist to this scenario: here's take two. So, Dan and Billy, neighboring pre-historic men make a plan to kill a wild boar for their families. Billy flushes, Dan pokes, Billy hacks, the boar is dead. The two men, exhausted, panting, kneel on opposite sides of the carcass, and Dan thinks: 'You know, if I didn't have Billy there, I could keep this whole thing for myself. And for my family. We'd get our strength back and . . . well, we could take a little to Billy's family.'"

"Spotting, out of the corner of his eye, a big limb fallen from a tree--a club really--he reaches over, grabs the club, beans Billy once, twice, however many times are necessary until blood gushes out of his ears. Billy's dead. Then some sort of judge comes along. And God says, 'There's a dead man here. Who's responsible for this wrong?'"

"Dan can say, 'not me, that stick did it,' and point to the club. But God's not so dumb; she knows someone held the stick; there's no one else around but Dan. There's still blood on his hands, isn't there, figuratively if not literally? Phroomp! Lightning, grease, end of story."

Curtis asks. "Moral?"

"Okay, okay. One more time with one more slight revision, and you get your moral. Suppose, after Dan talks to Billy but before the day of hunt, he remembers Carl, who, also hungry, lives up the creek past the boar's clearing. Dad happens to see Carl and says something like this: 'You know, Carl, you're not looking so good. Pretty thin there. The wife and kids? Um- hm, that's bad, that's too bad. By the way, I just mention this in passing, but Billy, down the way there, he and I have a little plan to kill that big boar who's out grazing in the clearing every morning. After we get him, he and I will split the meat--fifty-fifty.'"

"'Um-hm,' says Carl, interested."

"Dan senses Carl's eagerness. 'Between you and me, Carl, I'm not that fond of Billy, kind of self-centered, know what I mean? If something happened to him, an accident, say— nothing on purpose, of course!--I wouldn't feel that bad, really. Say, if about the time he just finished helping me kill that boar a--oh, I don't know--maybe a great big rock were to fall on his head and splatter his brains all over the ground--well, shoot, I'd have more meat than I need, know what I mean?'"

"'I do!' agreed Carl."

"'Well, hey, I've got to run, sharpen my spear and all. Best to the family.'"

"So, you can guess what happens: Billy, panting, on his knees, gets his head bashed in and brains spread across the ground by a rock that appears to have slipped out of Carl's hands. God shows up. 'There's a dead man here. Who's responsible for this wrong?' Dan can say, 'not me, that rock . . . or someone (nodding toward Carl) did it.' But God's not so dumb; she knows someone held the rock; and she knows--well, she knows everything of course; that's the way God works--she knows that Dan paid Carl to kill Billy."

Tim lingers on the word paid and then concludes. "There's still blood on both their hands, isn't there? Double phroomp!"

Curtis agrees. "Yes, blood on their hands, but I think you need to spell out the moral."

"What we've got here is the first ever voluntary military--Dan's paid killer force of one, Carl. You see, 'volunteer military' is our nice word for 'mercenaries,' but it's really what we have in America today. The non-soldiers, citizens in a democracy, taxpayers, pay others to kill people in exactly the same way Dan paid Carl to reduce Billy's head to mush."

"'Mercenaries' might be a bit strong. Yes, they are paid but most join in order to serve."

"Agreed. They're men and women willing to risk their lives to protect our way of life. Now, a lot of them join because they can't find a job where they live. Or they want to pay for their college education afterwards with the GI Bill. Or their parents know they need a little straightening out. But they all deserve our respect. So, I go to the parades, join in the singing of the national anthem, work with local veterans' organizations to help the next generation returning from wars. A lot of Vietnam vets like you and me feel the kinship."

"I see. Those of us who served know we have blood on our hands. Those who didn't pretend they don't. You think we deserve a special recognition."

"Right on, brother."

Curtis concludes. "I see your point. And I believe I'm convinced."

Chapter Thirty-three: Risks

When Curtis received one more obituary of a class member, Tricia's grainy photo of the neighborhood basketball court took clearer shape as David Chambers. He hadn't known David well (though the original yearbook picture was familiar), but he was, sadly, a person everyone in the class would recognize. He'd been in a car that was hit by a freight train.

The Missouri-Pacific railroad tracks ran behind the houses on the north side of Limestone Drive in the Circle. Behind the homemade neighborhood basketball court was the cut through the hillside through which trains ran. Anywhere from forty to fifty feet deep, "the Cut" (it had its name) hid the trains' noise and made them invisible from street level. It was the darkness of the cut from which a shadow had moved in Curtis' memory.

Car accidents were generally the first appearance of death or serious injury for young people. Yes, they lost grandparents and senior neighbors, but when their contemporaries figured in instances of sudden, unanticipated tragedy, they were stunned. Later, Curtis would realize this confrontation with sudden death was a sad preparation for what some would later encounter in war.

Curtis now believes the faster speed of automobiles and the big highways like Route 66 contributed to a higher rate of accidents. Progress and regression.

The accident that crippled David—and caused injuries that probably led to an early death—occurred on a Saturday night when a lot of teenagers were cruising downtown and making stops at Fanny's Dairy Delite, the A & W Root Beer drive-in, and the Maid Rite. Curtis had been playing bridge at the Castle house at the time. As often happens in such circumstances, he remembers the conversation that was interrupted by a phone call with the news.

Bill, who was the gambler and either won big or gloriously lost, had, with his partner Cindy, just made a small slam. "And that's the rubber," he gloated.

Gathering the hands and studying the sequence of tricks, Susan asked her partner, Curtis, "How did he know the queen of diamonds would fall?"

Bill laughed. "It was a gamble, and I got lucky. Sometimes you have to take a risk."

Curtis was the most cautious of the four bridge players. He relied on fidelity to the bidding system and careful calculation of odds. Susan was a good partner for him, methodical and deliberate also. Cindy was a good partner for Bill, often exaggerating the value of her hand because he had the ability to get more from the cards than expected.

They heard Mrs. Castle pick up the phone in the kitchen, and the girls noticed that she was listening and not answering. Finally, she said, "Okay. I'll tell them."

The boys' mouths were full of the pretzels and potato chips, but they did notice how intently Cindy and Susan looked at her.

"There's been a car accident," she said. "A member of your class, and a neighbor of yours," she nodded toward Susan "is badly hurt."

They all had two sets of friends: school friends, generally in the same grade; and neighborhood friends, often group of different ages. Susan's older brother had been a good friend of David and had repeatedly tried to get her to go out with him.

The former star hitter on the baseball team would spend the rest of his life in a wheelchair. And his case was one of the many reasons Susan went on to become a doctor.

Curtis felt the tragedy less strongly than Susan, but the image of a boy hit by a train joined with a memory from his own experience. The obituary of David Chambers brought up the event one more time.

He and a couple of other boys had begun a game of dare out in the woods: jump off this high rock to the trail below; climb this skinny sapling and pull it down from the top; grab the boxcar ladder of a moving train, pull yourself up, and ride from point A to point B. Curtis knew he was acting foolishly, somewhat like characters in a popular newspaper comic strip.

Curtis read Lil' Abner every Sunday in the St. Louis paper. Al Capp's fictional Dogpatch, a village somewhere in Appalachia, was peopled by uneducated and ignorant hillbillies. Curtis' father had told him many people viewed the Ozarks of Southern Missouri and Northern Arkansas as another collection of Dogpatches. But he assured him Fairfield, a college town with many professional people, was not like the world of Daisy Mae and the Yokums.

Oscar also informed his son that that the comic strip author had lost a leg above the knee at the age of nine in a trolley accident. This was clearly a father's precautionary tale. Curtis understood that his father would never have attempted such a foolish maneuver when he was a boy. And his son was never to try to hitch a ride on a train.

Years later, however, Curtis would overhear Oscar laughing about how he'd often caught an unauthorized train trip across the flat landscape of his Kansas childhood. He was, he thought, more open with his children, hoping to prevent their having to rewrite his life story when unacknowledged became known.

In phase four of the game of dare, the challenge was to hitch a ride on a train car. Curtis was running on the gravel bed of the railroad tracks when he saw his friend Donny Lawrence, several car lengths ahead of him, grab a rung of a boxcar ladder.

Donny held on by one hand and tried to reach up with

a second, but missed. Hanging by the grip of one hand, he swung his foot up to reach the bottom rung. Curtis gasped when it bounced off the boxcar's rear axle, though it was not caught between wheel and rail. The boys jumped off the railroad bed and raced into the woods, panting.

Curtis knew that several times on the way of his life's journey from Point A to Point B, he'd been lucky to escape crippling injury or an early end. And what he saw in Tricia's photo was the image of Donny's foot bouncing off the boxcar's steel wheel. Taking a goofy walk in the woods during his first reunion planning meeting he'd had to clamber down the railroad embankment to avoid detection. The image of Donny in danger of losing a limb was likely recalled.

When he and Beth checked in at the Midwest Mother Road Motel on the Thursday of the reunion weekend (Carol and Mark would arrive with his mother the next day), he was determined to return all such haunting images to the darkened corners of his subconscious. He wanted to satisfy Beth's desire that the event look forward more than it lingered over the past.

Barbara Lemon had picked up the copies of *Confluence II* from Fairfield Printing, so he believed his official duties had been completed and the weekend would be deeply satisfying. He did, however, have some unofficial duties to perform.

Patrick had arrived before him to begin the final phase of the scholarship drive. They'd talked by phone the week before. "You'll be happy to know," he informed Curtis, "we're at $2,500 for a boy, $2,700 for a girl. When I make the big announcement Friday night, I expect the competition to shift into high gear."

They'd talked to about twenty classmates they believed would jumpstart the campaign and were surprised but pleased at how much came in so quickly. Patrick also told Curtis about a confrontation he'd learned about indirectly. Susan Howe had been offended to hear one classmate tell her that he "didn't want the money he'd earned—and paid taxes on—to go to someone 'not an American.'"

Susan knew he meant a hyphenated American. So, without referring specifically to him, she sent a letter to classmates about America as a nation of immigrants and the cowardice of xenophobia behind the rising desire to restrict citizenship to people "just like us."

Curtis assumed that John Robinson's salacious proposal to Janet of a large donation for a rendezvous had not been accepted. But he felt it had been made. In one email to Curtis Janet had included a cryptic postscript—"So, you're John's pimp now?"—but followed it with a smiley face—":)"— and a promise to "tell all" in Fairfield.

Tim Carlson had invited all veterans and their spouses who could come to a pre-reunion brunch at the Table. Beth had heard so many of their tales from Curtis that she was eager to meet them. She might have suspected that a process of unpacking contradictions in Curtis' vision of the reunion would begin quickly, and that she might want to be with him as it proceeded.

They found a place to sit next to Roger, the geologist Curtis had met at a America's Main Street Diner, and his wife Lynne. They'd been immediate supporters of the scholarship idea, and Curtis suspected he'd sold the idea to a lot of his fellow retirees from the US Geological Survey. Not all of them had been able to afford college but probably knew a good career without that diploma was harder for the next generation.

While pizza was being prepared, Lynne tapped a spoon on her glass and requested the floor. She had, she said, something on her mind she had wanted to share and was going to do so with those she thought would understand.

She had been a civilian journalist with *Stars and Stripes* and had done two tours in Vietnam. "I think I have a sympathetic audience here, but, be warned, this might offend some. I think I'm getting something off my chest that has bothered me for some time."

Chapter Thirty-four: Histories

Lynne explained how she and Roger had lived for ten years in the quiet riverside neighborhood of Jericho, south of Cape Girardeau. "We always had a block party on Independence Day. And, like everyone else, I appreciated the basics--hot dogs, coleslaw, and beer--as well as the homemade desserts brought by my neighbors. But I couldn't quite pinpoint the source of those little twinges of anxiety that came each year with the event."

"You're not going to tell us you have bad memories of our Fairfield 4th of July picnic at Lions Club Park, are you?" asked Gary. They'd all had great fun at the annual celebration, which included a traveling set of rides—Ferris wheel, merry-go-round, tilt-a-wheel. "I don't want anything breaking the spell of the weekend." Beth raised her eyebrows.

"No, the problem comes from a different time. Roger came in after work one June day to announce that there would be a crawfish boil that year. And the fact that crawfish, though smaller, are related to lobster brought it back: forty years earlier, the Fourth of July, a beach on the South China Sea. I was afraid it was going to happen again: patriotism run amok déjà vu."

Curtis admitted, "Small towns can get excited about traditional holidays. Not always a bad thing."

"Not at all," agreed Lynne. "This was a personal issue. At Long Bihn we—I really mean the men—would build charcoal fires in fifty-gallon drums cut in half and then boil lobster to celebrate any holiday. One of the Army reporters would use his press pass to hop a ride down to Vung Tau and come back with half a dozen crates of live South China sea lobsters."

"Life in the rear of a war zone," admitted Gary.

"And, of course, there was also plenty of beer as the enlisted men pooled their monthly rations to build up a stockpile. And the mess hall made enough coleslaw to . . . well, to feed an army. So everything necessary to a party was there. No one anticipated the explosion of pent-up feelings that resulted. Or the other explosion."

The group was quieter and listened more closely. She shifted the scene of her narrative back to Missouri and the recent time.

"Now, in Jericho there are only about twenty homes, a small community mostly inhabited by retirees who'd grown up in the area, had plenty of money, and didn't want to take their accumulated wealth to Florida or Arizona. There was an unspoken assertion among them that, residing in the middle of the country--only a few hundred yards, in fact, from the Mississippi River--Jericho represented the very center of the nation."

"Can I guess," interrupted Tim, "that Jericho residents put up American flags in every configuration: off a porch column slanting up and away; horizontally displayed in windows or vertically above the garage door; hoisted by rope and pulley to the top of a pole?"

"You may. Now, Roger and I were recent comers to Jericho. And I'd made a few unfortunate comments about bumper stickers to a few of our neighbors. One retired bank president was objecting to things he'd read, obviously having made a list. 'Burn the women who won't Burn the Bra'; 'Fry Bush in Oil"; 'To Hell's Flames with Hate.' So, I said that it was just kids spouting off. They grow up, at least most of them do."

"But the guy said, 'They see those inflammatory statements and get the idea it's all right to blow up a school or a hospital. I say the state police ought to be allowed to inspect the cars of such hooligans."

Curtis chuckled. "He was overestimating their capacity for genuine action. But some of the less offensive bumper stickers still get me hot, as if a slick saying on your car is an adequate answer to the world's problems."

Lynne nodded. "I made the mistake of objecting to 'Support the Troops' as just too easy. Then I remembered that most of the Jericho folks our age had some kind of deferment to avoid the draft. And you all know, only a handful of elected officials in Washington have relatives in the service. But they're the first propose more ceremonies to honor the troops."

Jimmy nodded. "They think that, and a yellow ribbon, will save the country after 9/11."

Lynne went on, returning to the lobster roast in Vietnam. "You know, I'd never eaten lobster and was not pleased to watch the wiggling live creatures dropped headfirst into boiling water, even though the guy cooking—a cook, in fact—-assured me they didn't feel a thing--death was so quick, and they had primitive nervous systems anyway."

Curtis added. "When they're in the boiling water, you can pick up a high-pitched sound, as if the lobsters are crying. But

I'm told, that's just gas coming through their shells."

Gary chuckled. "When any novice asks if here's no pain, the pros always say, not unless you let them get your fingers with their pincers or spill the water on your privates."

Curtis remembered stepping out of a jet plane onto the steaming dark tarmac at Cam Rahn Bay Air Force Base. He was amazed he didn't melt on the spot.

Lynne gave a big sigh. "In Jericho, while their houses were not directly on the water, we shared ownership of several acres along the shore and a path, usable in most seasons, down from the low hills to a sandy beach. That's where they set off the fireworks every year."

Curtis noted that she'd changed from using the personal pronoun "we" to the generic "they."

"The neighbors milled around our large gazebo where they would watch the fireworks as soon as dusk was a bit deeper. A few were still suffering tears and runny noses, as the cooks had insisted on authentically spicy pepper seasoning for the crawfish. One woman's fingers had gotten too close to her eyes at one point, so she'd had to retreat to a nearby house and flush them with cold water."

Jimmy shook his head. "I don't know about the rest of you, I'm not an enthusiast for fireworks these days."

"Funny you should say that," said Lynne. "I had asked if we might consider celebrating without fireworks. The suggestion was not well received. I remember one guy saying something like, 'What do mean, something other than fireworks? It's Fourth of July, man! We'd be the only town in the U.S. of A. not lighting up the sky in celebration of our nation's birth.'"

"I pointed out that it was expensive, dangerous."

Gary agreed. "Every year you read about some kid blowing off his fingers or burning down a barn. As the mayor, I've had to console parents and siblings too many times."

Lynne nodded. "Unfortunately, we didn't have a good alternative: balloons, confetti, a lawnmower parade?"

"So, Curtis asked, "after you'd boiled crawfish (and heard their little cries), your neighbors set the sky on fire?"

"Well, we had, as I was told, exploding stars, ground bloom clusters, Roman candles, multi-break shells, Bengal fires, horsetails, spiders, crossettes, time rains. The show went on for over half an hour. Everyone turned around to ooh and ahh at multi-colored streaks of light, bright rising wheels, and spinning galaxies of fire."

"I hope this story has a happy ending," said Jimmy.

Again, Lynne sighed. "There were no casualties this time. But that wasn't the case at that lobster feast in Long Bihn. You all know we big guns over there that worked day and night throughout Vietnam, churning up distant countryside, decimating enemy camps, razing jungle used for cover."

"We had the firepower hands down," Roger admitted. "But we never won the hearts and minds."

Lynne nodded. "Charlie's hand-carried rockets and mortars were like toys in comparison, but when one shell hit the oil truck that Fourth of July, four men were burned to a crisp. Dumb curiosity had made me wander down to the site when the fires were dying down and the intense heat had gone down. The bodies were covered with ponchos, but, as one was lifted onto a stretcher, the cover slipped off. I saw what looked like an oversized hot dog that had fallen through the grill and been left on the coals for hours."

"Shee-it," said Gary softly. The others shivered, possible recalling their own memories of war's casualties.

"In Jericho that night, when one of our asshole neighbors— in a brief gap between the whooshes, the bangs, and the ratta-tat-tats—began to sing 'God Bless America.,' I kind of lost it. The voices rose into the night, and new streaks of smoke trailed projectiles up into the sky. All that noise and spectacle and light hid too many things I could never explain."

As with one voice the phrase, "There it is," rose from the group.

None of the vets or spouses would go to Carol Yates' fireworks display that night.

Chapter Thirty-five: Roots

Curtis was moved to offer a footnote to Lynne's story. "I have a friend—well, an acquaintance—who's a Vietnam vet, and he gets hot when those who didn't serve hold forth about what we should have done, what we did wrong, etc. If there's time . . ."

The server came to offer coffee refills, and most cups were raised. So, Curtis went on. "It won't excuse that arrogance or ignorance, but it helps me put it in context. I was working the soda fountain at Hillcrest Drugs one day when Jeanne Duncan bumped into me, causing me to splash milkshake onto the counter in front of a customer."

"Jeanne Duncan?" questioned Tim. "I don't remember her."

"No, not in any class at Fairfield High; but that's part of the reason I tell about this incident—to show how ignorant I was of circles outside our own."

Beth chimed in. "Oh, he's still ignorant of lots of things. But I know this story. It's worth hearing."

"Thank you, dear," Curtis smiled. "So, 'Hey,' I said to Jeanne softly, not wanting to draw customers' attention but registering my surprise and my sense of insult. I was startled because Jeanne and I worked well together, trading workplace duties easily and never getting in each other's way. My surprise increased because she did not acknowledge the collision or offer even a cursory 'I'm sorry.'"

"Sounds rude to me," offered Sandra.

"'I'm sorry,' I said to the customer, setting the metal milk-shake container back on the mixer and taking a towel to wipe up the spill. At the same time I watched what Jeanne did next, which was to lean close to a young man sitting on the short "L" leg of the counter, either to ask him something or to listen to something he has to say."

"Ah, your rival," suggested Gary.

"In a sense, yes. But this hip bump—unconscious on Jeanne's part, I will come to understand—is for me, I now know, an important event in a painfully slow adolescent discovery of sex. The hip jolt has also become a landmark in my confrontation with death, but I won't feel its full impact until many years have passed."

Curtis paused and rubbed his chin. "'What was that?' I asked Jeanne when the rush had slowed and we were washing and drying dishes together at the soda fountain's double sink."

"She turned toward me with a friendly smile. 'What was what?'"

"'Why, you went behind me there and made me spill milk-shake.'"

"She appeared genuinely puzzled. 'Made me spill?'"

"It hurt even more to realize she was completely unaware of the accident, of a girl bumping into a boy. You see, I was no more masculine to her than an ice cream freezer."

There was the expected chorus of ah's and oh's.

"Thank you, thank you. But, you see, Jeanne's matter-of-fact response to physical contact was, I believed, a product of the post-high school experience I only dreamed of. And—listen to this—the distance between my innocence and Jeanne's sophistication was underscored by her upper Midwest pronunciation of a few words, one especially common in soda fountain jargon: 'root beer.' Everyone I know has always said the first word to rhyme with 'boot'; but Jeanne pronounced it to rhyme with 'put.'"

They all echoed the two sounds and concluded that "root" was "boot."

"How odd her 'root' was," Curtis continued, "but how suggestive. Now, I make no pun here with the word 'root' referring to a man's, um, manhood. But I will come to see other meanings in the 'beer' half of that soft drink's name later, too. My plan that Saturday morning had simply been to pour the milkshake into a Coke glass and deliver it to Gayle Thomas—remember her, two years behind us?—who was prettily perched on one of the counter stools. Now I had to recover both the milkshake and my composure."

Another chorus of mock sympathy.

"When I started at Hillcrest, I felt it was the best possible time to begin experiencing the pleasures someone older, like Jeanne, knew. There are other occasions in my life when I arrived at the worst possible time. That's where I'm heading in this story. Farewell, Robert Duncan."

"But back on that fateful Saturday morning I was wiping up spilled milkshake, putting the metal mixing container back on the machine, and demanding to know why my co-worker seems oblivious to my presence. 'Oh,' she finally said, grinning. 'Was it when I served that very attractive young man at the end of the counter?'"

"Was he attractive?" Curtis shrugged. "My head stayed with the hip that had bumped me. Jeanne laughed, squeezing my arm. 'That was my husband. He's stationed at Fort Wood. That's why I'm here.'"

"You never thought she might be married?" asked Roger.

"Well, to tell the truth, clues had surfaced in our casual conversations. She'd moved here from North Dakota for no reason I knew. Yet I knew women sometimes stayed in the area while their fiancés or husbands trained to be Army engineers. But I didn't connect any dots. I understood Jeanne only as part of my world, rather than as belonging to a different one."

Tim grinned. "Ah, you came, that is to say, from different roots (roots rhyming with 'boots,' not 'foots')."

"Ah-ha! Right. While my father had worked for the Navy at Oak Ridge National Laboratory during the war, he returned to his chosen career when it was over. Jeanne was from a military family Three generations—grandfather, father and uncles, brother."

Jimmy admitted, "A lot of us draftees didn't reclassify

ourselves mentally from 'civilian' to 'military.' I saw myself within the framework of a middle-class life—high school, college, professional careers. We had a naive belief that events far away—those we associate with the making of history— would have no effect on us in our comfortable stateside life."

"I saw how the world outside America affected others in the summer after my freshman year," admitted Curtis. "I signed on with a United States Geological Survey team headed for northern North Dakota." He smiled at Roger. "I would shoulder the 15-foot survey pole (it folded in half at the 8-foot point) and hoist it on low and high spots in the ground so that a trained geologist like our friend Roger could use his sextant to map a portion of the plains too level to reveal its contours in aerial photographs."

"On the way home that August I made a stop to change buses in Fargo and, on a whim, looked into the city phone book, found a number, and called Jeanne."

"A bold move," Tim said. "Not exactly what I would have expected from you. Sorry, Beth, he must have developed his romantic skills after high school."

She smiled. "Oh, I knew I'd found a rough-cut jewel. A diamond now, of course."

Curtis went on. "Jeanne had certainly never anticipated receiving a call from her former fellow soda fountain worker. She said—with a hesitation I brushed aside—that she would be at home and I could stop by, 'if I wanted to.'"

"Ten minutes later she stepped out onto the stoop of a one-story frame house, a small, slender woman folding her arms around herself against the wind of the northern prairie, chilly some days even in the summer. Her hair was cut short, and she wore an inexpensive skirt and blouse, not the stylish slacks or dresses of the women who went to school with me.

There was a hollowed look around her eyes, though, which did strike me as unusual.

Lynne cocked her head "You're about to learn something, I suspect."

He nodded. "I only had an hour between buses (and less time at her house), so not much of substance was communicated from her to me or me to her—until the last moment. Self-absorbed as 19-year-old males tend to be, I didn't ask if she was living alone, back home with her family, or had roommates sharing expenses. The 'attractive' young man she'd identified as her soldier husband was nowhere to be seen."

Several "uh-oh's" sounded.

"That Robert Duncan had been reported 'missing in action' in Vietnam just days before I showed up at her home didn't register in my vision of how Americans lived and loved and worked. Nor did it alter my sense of my own identity or social commitment—until recently."

He nodded at Gary, who said, "Old soldiers."

"'Root' as in 'put,'" offered Sandra.

Curtis sighed. "That's also how the other part of 'root beer was redefined for me: 'bier'—a stand on which a coffin is placed."

Chapter 36: Slam

When he had confirmed with Barbara that *Confluence II* had been printed, Curtis began to focus, not on the event of playing bridge, but on the game itself. Because he'd hadn't touched a deck in years, he began to wonder if he still knew strategy. Imagining cards dealt and spread out among four hands, he had trouble anticipating the bidding, the play, the scoring.

In between the brunch and the early evening social hour/ get together, he asked Beth what she could remember about playing bridge. "What? You haven't forgotten yourself, have you?"

His hesitation gave him away. "Well, . . . "

They were stretched out on the bed, still a bit weary from the flight, the reunion of siblings and mother in St. Louis, the emotional energy of the veterans' shared experience.

"Good grief!" she exclaimed. "All that planning, cajoling, bullying the others, and you don't even know how to play the game. We haven't sat down at a bridge table for decades, even though you've continued to pester me to join a group."

"Well, as you know, you never took the game that seriously. And I guess your casual attitude wore off on me to the degree that . . . that I've lost my edge."

"Lost your . . . !" She rolled her eyes.

He was right, though: bridge for Beth was a social event, not a competition. They'd left many rubbers half finished because, during a hand, she and one or two others got caught up in conversation and never picked up the game where it had been left off. He would be haunted by the potential of masterful play, a small or a grand slam.

"I'm sure it's like riding a bike. Once the game starts, it'll come back to me . . . I think."

"All right," she sighed and sat up on the bed. "Why don't we deal a few hands, leave them face up on the table, and go over the basics."

"We don't . . . " He was going to say that they had no cards, but Beth stepped over to her open suitcase and pulled out two matching decks. "Cards!" he exclaimed. "You never cease to amaze me."

"As long as we've been married, I think I know you: strengths and weaknesses. You move forward with a project but then realize you have to backtrack, prepare better, and begin again. I foresaw this situation and planned accordingly."

Their children as well had recognized the dynamics of the couple's union: his impulsive, at times contagious, enthusiasm; her deliberate, steady patience. Their musician son Justin was like his father. Carl, after a rebellious youth, developed the balance and composure of Beth. And Mary Anne, their architect, balanced the opposing traits.

Curtis couldn't blame Beth on her plan to prep him for the event. His success in promoting Bridge Déjà Vu had resulted in him having to review something that had once been automatic. Using a stock phrase from real estate, he realized she was "upgrading" one room in his old brain.

"You're saying you have a small slam?" said his partner Susan later that afternoon. He'd made the bid, and their opponents, Cindy and Bill, didn't know if they should double. They also didn't know if Susan was tempting them to challenge the contract when she knew they had it.

"Well, I have read quite a few books about bridge," smiled Curtis coyly. He was enjoying the risk of his bid. Unlike in adolescence, where failure could be difficult, here it would just lead to laughter.

Looking up at Bill, Cindy said, "It wasn't books that taught us bookworms how to play bridge: it was your mom."

He smiled. "She loved to play, but never took the game too seriously. That may be the key to enjoying the game."

"I can go along with that," agreed Susan. "I got in a bridge club in medical school, and it was cutthroat—whoops. Bad pun for doctors. Anyway, individuals have to decide if they enjoy the company or the game." She raised a hand. "I trust we're going to remain friends tonight!"

Curtis interpreted their chuckles as another good step in the recovery of old friendships, the goal of his scheme. But he felt Bill's grin had a hint of more than laughter.

"You know," Bill said, "I'm the only one of you who returned to Fairfield to stay. So, the friend you had then should pretty much match the one you see here. You guys, on the other hand, have left your hometown, travelled, and lived elsewhere. Who knows who you've become and if we can now be friends?"

Cindy said, "I think Curtis is right, though. You learn a lot about another person when you share an activity like playing bridge. Good and bad traits come to the surface, and you begin to learn what kind of person the other guy is."

"In that case," responded Bill. "I double your bid."

So, the game was played. But as he struggled to make the bid, Curtis thought again about Bill's high school project of identifying the town's sewage system. He saw in his mind the map Bill had unrolled in his cabin and the strange account of a ghostly descendant of a Trail of Tears. Had he prepared some bizarre surprise for the reunion?

It wasn't exactly true that Curtis had read a lot about playing bridge. When they were learning back in high school, he'd found an introductory book in Fairfield Public Library: *Bridgework*. (The title now had a different meaning for him and his fellow seniors!) He'd studied it intensely.

A week before they left North Carolina, he located a copy on E-Bay, used his PayPal account to purchase it from a collector in British Columbia, and had it in his hands in two days. When Beth saw it, of course, she complained it was another step into the past rather than a move toward the future.

As it happened, a situation similar to the one he was in against Bill and Cindy had been a sample game explained in detail in *Bridgework*. It involved a risky gamble: losing a trick in the trump suit early to make your opponents think they would sink the bid easily. But Curtis took every trick after that.

"Well played," admitted Cindy. "But we're just getting started."

"And" grinned Bill, "who knows what unexpected events are in store for us?"

Susan's eyes widened as she looked across the table at Curtis. He'd written her about his visit with Bill, so she was probably thinking the same thing he was: Bill had planned something.

After Curtis refilled drinks—all non-alcoholic, as this crowd had gone from college boozing to social drinking to virtual abstinence—Bill asked, "Do you all remember doing—or trying to do—the Twist?"

This was the first dance in their lifetime when partners didn't touch, just rotated their hips and shoulders in time with the beat. The music, rock-in-roll, featured a more pronounced beat than did Big Band music, which had spawned the jitterbug. Curtis remembered several girls whose hips were (he punned) hypnotic.

"I recall couples doing it at the senior prom, but I couldn't get it right. But why do you ask? I don't remember you as a star on the dance floor. No offense, of course: none of us was."

"No reason," answered Bill. "It's just another of those images that has popped up in connection to the reunion. Chubby Checker and the Twist."

Curtis said, "Something else popped up for me: Sonja Jones's story in the yearbook."

Susan said, "I remember her from 4-H. Really very smart. I'm sorry I lost track of her after we graduated."

"Well, she's more than fulfilled any promise: degree in Agriculture, Peace Corps volunteer, worked in the State Department."

Cindy squinted. "I don't really remember her."

Curtis admitted. "She was black, and I'm embarrassed to admit she must have been invisible to me. There were so few, and we must have been in different tracks in school. I'm hoping to get a chance to talk to her this weekend."

He did, but Beth even more. And what she found changed the landscape of the class yet again.

Chapter Thirty-seven: Prophecy

Each table at the reunion dinner seated ten. Curtis, Beth, and his mother Mid joined Sandra, Janet and her husband Stanley, Mayor Jimmy and his wife Rebecca (from the class after theirs), Sonja and her husband Douglas.

Settled with their drinks (iced tea or water) and following introductions, Mid leaned across the table to speak to Janet. "Curtis tells me you've been a great ally both in organizing this event and . . . "—I hope it's okay to say in this group—"getting contributions to the scholarship drive."

Janet laughed, "I am but one of your son's fellow schemers. Everyone at this table has played a part."

Mid went on. "I sense that you and a number of others felt that helping the next generation was more important than celebrating your own. Do you have special motivation?"

Again, Janet laughed. "To tell you the truth, I was inspired by 'The Voice of God.'"

Curtis said, "I've heard a lot of stories leading up to and at this reunion, but none about a prophet. Please tell."

"Okay. This is not going to be exactly the testimony you might hear at a . . . um, fundamentalist church event. No offense to anyone. I'm Catholic, by the way."

"None taken," said Sandra. "This is, I believe, an ecumenical group. I, for instance, am Jewish. I know Jimmy and Becky are Methodist. Sonja?"

"Raised Baptist, now Muslim."

"Ah," said Janet, "with Curtis and family Episcopalian, we've got a lot of bases covered." She leaned forward to all could hear. "So, for years I have sung in a community chorus, about fifty folks who came together twice a year to offer good will concerts. Our director recruits soloists, who rehearse separately. The rest of us amateurs come from church choirs."

Sonja nodded. "I do the same thing in New York. In times of trouble—post-9/11 for instance—these events can be healing, unifying."

Jimmy agreed. "Yes, at least for a time. Still, I'm grateful even if the effect is brief."

Janet went on, "Well, a few years year ago, at our spring concert, the first time the soloists came to our rehearsal, the soprano's voice struck me so profoundly it sent chills down my spine. I hadn't seen her because she had entered from the back of the sanctuary and was singing from the pulpit, above and behind me. She was, I concluded, 'The Voice of God.'"

"What was the piece?" asked Beth, who also sang in her church choir.

"Ralph Vaughan William's 'Dona Nobis Pacem—Grant us Peace.'"

"Beginning of the first movement?" asked Sandra. "When the soprano comes in on top of the orchestra and choir? I've got a recording of that somewhere—it's beautiful."

"Exactly. It's a powerful moment, and . . . well, that day I felt that the words spoke to me, to our community, to the nation."

Beth recited thoughtfully. "'O Lamb of God, who takes away the sins of the world, have mercy upon us.' Sadly, although we're a nation of many accomplishments, we also have offenses that need forgiveness. Wasn't it composed in the 1930s, a time the world was headed for a second global war. So, there's certainly relevance in our time."

Janet nodded. "Yes. This performance was, I think, 2005, not long after 9/11 and when the conflict in Iraq had taken not just one but a number of ugly turns."

Curtis said with more energy than he'd meant to use, "Our generation had fought one war in Vietnam based on outmoded colonialist notions, and then we marched off and did the same thing all over again. It was dry where we were wet—about the only difference I saw."

Janet sighed. "We all were affected by that war—participants, anti-war protesters, family members. But this time, while soldiers and civilians were dying thousands of miles away, most Americans were going about business as usual. 'Go the mall,' we were told; enjoy the fruits of America's prosperity. I longed for some kind of wake-up call and felt it in the soprano's voice. Agnus Dei, qui tollis peccata mundi, misere. 'The Voice of God.'"

Jimmy said, "I bet your director was making a statement in choosing that piece."

Janet nodded. "Absolutely. At first, I didn't think the slender, tall brunette he'd brought in as a solo could be the prophet we needed--too young, too beautiful, too bright. I didn't know her, but another of the sopranos told me about her."

"She was a professional?"

"I'm not sure of her credentials exactly. Another soprano told me that Jennifer—that's the soloist's name—sang in their church choir but never mentioned that she'd had training. She molded her singing to match the other sopranos, asked for help with difficult or unusual passages, and sometimes laughed at her own goofs. They thought she was, as my friend said, 'just one of us,' But when her voice filled every crevice in the sanctuary—and pierced my heart—her fellow church members were as stunned as the rest of us."

Curtis reflected on such moments: an unassuming young woman transformed into a commanding presence. Was it possible that others across the land were calling the people to a new awareness? He asked Janet, "Isn't that the piece inspired by Walt Whitman?"

"Yes," she confirmed. "The text is from one of the nation's greatest poets. I looked all this up in preparing for the performance. Whitman's compassion for soldiers came from his service as a hospital volunteer in the American Civil War. Ralph Vaughan Williams, the composer, was a veteran of World War I. Their spirits came together in this lament about the costs of war."

Sandra said, "But, as you said earlier, we've created a society that compartmentalizes the costs of war. Soldiers and their families take it on without the rest of society understanding of how hard that is. Especially the multiple and sometimes back-to-back tours they are assigned in Iraq and Afghanistan. Lynne, Roger's wife, had a powerful story about that."

Janet added, "Jennifer understood, though. I talked to her after the final performance. She had put her musical career on hold while raising three small children. What surprised me even more—because she clearly has talent—is that she was thinking of going into nursing."

"I hope that's not because she was motivated by the good salaries in medicine and the conventional desire for expensive homes, cars, possessions," worried Jimmy. "That philosophy has spurred economic development in Fairfield, but not as much civic spirit as I'd like to see."

"Jennifer was inspired by having looked after her grandfather when he was dying in a nursing home. She told me we ought to do better in this country for those who are ill. She would have to go back to school first to get the right science courses, but planned to do that at night."

Curtis cautioned, "Nowadays that can take six years—even more."

Janet chuckled "I also told her she can't take care of everyone. But she just laughed and said, 'I'll care for them one at a time.'"

"She's a rare one," admitted Curtis. "Whitman's 'Dirge for Two Veterans,' part of the Dona Nobis Pacem, is about the sufferings of generations, which we may be losing sympathy for." He recited: "'I hear a sad procession, / And I hear the sound of coming full-keyed bugles. / Two veterans, son and father, dropped together/ And the double grave awaits them.' In our current wars a national guard father--or mother--might have a child, a soldier, in harm's way. Would we grieve their falling as we should?"

Janet said, "Jennifer's plan was to teach music appreciation online at the community college to earn her own tuition. She would get most of that homework done in the evenings."

Beth said, "That's a determined woman. And a model for her generation."

"If you ask me," said Sandra, "someone ought to write about Whitman and Williams, about citizen soldiers and shared sacrifice. Would it change the world? Probably not, but maybe our task now is to change people, as your friend Jennifer says, 'one at a time'."

Mid must have decided another generation's voice had to be heard. "I've seen this before, friends: in the Depression, in World War II, even in the Cold War. Communities across the country shared awareness and purpose. The media could right now decide to give more time to things like Wounded Warriors and programs designed to support their families, to the case for spending more on healthcare—civilian and military. If we were focused on things like that, fewer people would be looking for the next war, for the next chance to demonize a person or a group, for yet more sophisticated weapons of mass destruction." She sighed. "It could happen."

Her summary brought a silence to the group. So, she declared, "It may be idealistic to see peace on earth in my, or my children's, or my grandchildren's', or my great grand childrens' lifetime. But tonight, nodding at Janet, we have heard 'The Voice of God.' Let us all believe."

Chapter Thirty-eight: Twist

"What the hell is this?" exploded John Robinson. He marched across the banquet room holding his copy of *Confluence II*, from which, it seemed, he had pulled a pamphlet or brochure.

Curtis stared. Across the top of the document, he saw the words "Déjà Vu: a Twist" in large print; it was a headline, it seemed, to text and pictures that appeared below and continued on the back. He took the flyer. "I've never seen this before. It was in the yearbook?"

"It's in every copy. Your idea of a joke, a twisted joke, if you ask me."

Half a dozen other classmates, led by Barbara Lemon, also holding copies of the flyer, were gathering behind Robinson. Curtis had distributed a copy to each classmate at the evening event, proudly circling among the tables.

"Let me look," he said. "The printer must have mixed up his jobs and included this . . . whatever it is . . . in our book by accident."

It wasn't a real estate brochure, credit card offer, or municipal announcement. It was a broadsheet review of a movie, *Dr. Strangelove Déjà Vu*. Curtis began reading aloud to the group.

"The remake of *Dr. Strangelove: or How I Learned to Stop Worrying and Love the Bomb* has none of the force of the original. Start with the cast—gone in whatever nuclear Armageddon followed the end of the classic version, all but a few to their real graves.

Still, John Robinson [his yearbook picture had been inserted] portrays with uncanny commitment the looney Air Force general John D. Ripper ordering nuclear strikes against Iraq, Iran, and other Muslim countries of the Middle East. His conviction that Islamic terrorists are intent on robbing the "precious bodily fluids" of American men via "physical acts of love" seems genuine, even though he appears to want to eject his own with any willing partner.

Turning the brochure over, Curtis stopped reading. "This is Bill Castle's doing. He wrote it and somehow got someone at the printers to slip one in each copy. We have to make an announcement. Get everyone to discard it. It's a joke."

"I'm not amused," said John angrily.

"Nor am I," added Barbara. "You two were friends. Are you sure you didn't work with him to sabotage the reunion?"

"Hey! You know how hard I worked on *Confluence II*. Come on, John; get any inserts out of the remaining copies, and I'll make an announcement."

Over the PA system Curtis apologized for the mix-up. He noticed some classmates were not giving up their copies but reading and chuckling, pointing to pictures and reading passages out loud. When he returned to his table and read more, he saw that Bill had done a *Mad* comic version of the reunion couched in the storyline of the famous Cold War satire. It was funny, Curtis realized, even though he himself was credited with playing the evil genius of the title.

He tried not to laugh himself as he read.

Major Kong, this time a woman [Barbara Lemon, picture], a.k.a. Queen Kong, appears to be willing to gather bodily fluids. Because of chaos in the chain of command, though, she ends up riding a nuclear armed missile (not the general's) headed toward Moscow.

With "mutual assured destruction" looming, crippled former Nazi Dr. Strangebloom recommends utilizing underground mines, tunnels, and large sewage pipes to protect chosen Americans from the coming holocaust. He proposes one thousand—with a fifty female to one male ratio—be assigned to live below the surface for the next decade and repopulate the earth. At this prospect General Ripper gleams.

Dr Strangebloom, an odd gleam in his eyes, adds, "It could be kind of a class reunion—West Point, Annapolis, Air Force Academy, Fairfield High guys. We were all nurtured, you know, in a distinctive environment: patriotic, scientific, progress oriented."

Apparently, the Sexual Revolution has come early to this movie's military, however, and Miss Scott, secretary in the 1960s version, cut Strangebloom off. "All you boys wanted to do back then was pull out your guns at home and in Vietnam. Your sons and grandsons are doing it now in Iraq and Afghanistan. And the girls back home are getting penetrated as always."

She announces that only one man, holder of millions of sperm, is needed to multiply homo sapiens in the bowls of the earth.

When the generals ask who the lone male is, she explains that an alum from the Fairfield (Missouri) High School of fifty years ago has already been chosen. His history of ruthless conquest reveals a genetic capacity to continue tyranny on the planet. Shackles and electric shock, however, will be used to keep him on task.

But [the review concludes] "it would be wrong to include in this movie review such a spoiler. So, all likely candidates for all roles, gird your loins for a new future."

The mock review included a reproduction of Bill's high school map of the Fairfield sewer system, X's marking key locations for the colony's projected institutions—schools, factories, medical facilities.

He had to ask Janet, who was sitting at the same table with him and Beth, "Tell me there's no way Bill could have learned about John Robinson's . . . um . . . proposal to you. It's pretty clear he was cast as the villain—or one of them—in his piece."

She laughed. "I certainly never leaked it, though there are some uncanny parallels."

"Proposal?" smiled Beth. Curtis had told her about the deal and knew that Janet had also informed her husband, Stanley.

Janet admitted that John had offered to write a a big check to the scholarship fund for a night of her . . .company.

She laughed. "It was just as you predicted: dinner, dancing, and whatever at some swank hotel, probably one down by the Arch in St. Louis, and he would bankroll the project."

"According to Patrick, no check of that size has been received. So, you turned him down?"

"Oh, well, I proposed a different deal."

"I need to hear about that!"

Susan came up to join the conversation. "I haven't heard all of this, but it sounds as if there might have been some strange goings on in the reunion planning. I'm kind of glad I was out of town for it all."

"I was out of town, too," complained Curtis, "but found myself in the middle of a number of . . . um, disagreements."

Susan unfolded her copy of *Déjà Vu: A Twist,* the map side facing them. "You say he drew this up as a science fair project our senior year? Looks as if it's been updated."

"Right. Bill showed me the original when I visited him last summer. This is more detailed, quite meticulous. Well, he was always that way."

Jimmy, the mayor, joined them. "I've been studying this map If you look closely, some of the letters on the map are slightly darker than others—just one or two in a street name, a business, a municipal building."

"An accident in drawing and labeling?" asked Susan.

"I don't think so. Start up here at the top, noon, and go clockwise in smaller and smaller circles until you end up at the center of town, the nexus also of our sewer system."

Beth started to connect the letters and read. "F-R-O-M T-H-E F-R-I-N-G-E-S D-O-W-N T-O T-H-E C-E-N-T-E-R O-F O-U-R F-A-I-R T-O-W-N, M-A-Y T-R-U-E P-E-A-C-E A-B-O-U-N-D."

"Good grief—it's a haiku—seventeen syllables." He read it again, pausing to emphasize the three-line structure. "A bit corny, maybe, but . . ."

"There's this also," insisted Jimmy, tapping the map. "It appears to be some sort of plan to deal with natural disasters—tornados, long-term loss of electric power, even, God forbid, military attack. The subtitle—you can see it right here—is 'Safe Haven.'"

Cindy said, "I noticed he used colors in a pattern I didn't quite see at first. And there are small arrows in some streets."

Jimmy explained. "I think entry points to the underground system are indicated in blue, unusable sections in red, connecting routes in green. I'm going to pass this on to the town manager and town council. We don't ever want anything bad to threaten the town, but there may be some things we can learn from this scheme."

"So, even if we were scattered," said Curtis, "we could be reunited by *Déjà Vu: A Twist*."

"Nice," admitted Sandra.

"I haven't seen Bill," said Janet. "Was he coming? Anybody know?"

Curtis admitted, "To tell the truth, I'm still afraid he's engineered some grand entrance. Or, worse, some smoke bomb, or stink bomb, to be released when Jimmy makes his 'Key to the City' address."

Chapter Thirty-nine: Heads

Before Jimmy's presentation and a welcoming speech from Steve Carter, the class president, Mid asked how Janet had dealt with John's salacious proposal. "Curtis has told me you're a weaver. So, your situation reminds me of Penelope's in *The Odyssey*."

Curtis agreed. "Odysseus's wife was a weaver, too, manipulating the men who wanted her to admit her husband had died after the Trojan war. She had, they claimed, to choose one of them as the next king of Ithaca. Penelope said when the shroud she was weaving for her husband was finished, she'd make her choice. But every night she undid what she'd done by day. She threaded the men of the court into a new structure."

"That compares my little ruse to one of much, much more importance," said Janet. "She was saving the realm, and I was just having some fun. You see, all I said to John was that I wanted to take pictures. To be able to prove I slept with the greatest lover of our class."

"Well," laughed Mid, "His picture was taken—and included in *Déjà Vu: A Twist*."

Curtis thought Mid winked at Janet, as if she knew more about Dr. Strangebloom than he thought. Could she have been a co-conspirator with Bill? He dismissed the idea as Steve, a retired cardiologist, began his welcome to the class.

"When my family moved to Fairfield—I was just nine—I was pretty much a loner. This sometimes fierce independence came from my father, a Midwestern physicist, only son of a Swedish immigrant, who would join no organization, social, political, religious. Not many of you would have met him, given his private manner."

Curtis understood that this man resembled his own father.

Steve went on. "My mother, from a stoic New England family, could join or not join; she just put her head down and did what needed to be done."

Curtis remembered Steve being quite social, hardly a loner. He didn't know him until seventh grade, though, when kids from East and West Elementary went to the same junior high school, which was located in the old high school building. It hadn't been able to handle the increasing population of future baby boomers, so a new school was built.

"This insistence on self-reliance was absorbed by me on many occasions. One was when, like other kids my age, I decided to join the Boy Scouts." There were nods around the hall, suggesting that most had followed a similar path to Girl or Boy Scouts.

"My parents didn't discourage me, but, when I came home from an early meeting and announced with great excitement that we were going to get to make our own canoe paddles, my father, from his easy chair throne in the living room, nodded thoughtfully, Then, tapping the fingertips of one hand against the fingertips of the other—a characteristic gesture of this really philosophical man—he asked me, 'So,' he said, 'you have canoes?'"

Chuckles came from around the room.

Steve continued in a skilled imitation of a boy's voice. "'Well, of course . . . I mean I think so. I . . . '" More chuckles.

"In another characteristic gesture, my father raised one open hand to stop me and said, 'No matter. You can go on to making airplane propellers.'"

This time there was even more energetic laughter.

"In that single exchange my father showed me that human institutions are inherently flawed. And, a young boy, who worshipped his father, I believed him. But somewhere along the way after that, I began to test his assertion."

"I met a boy in my seventh-grade class who was much more outgoing than I was. He was from the other side of town, on Tenth Street close to the hospital."

Many nodded, suspecting that this was Tommy Benson, later identified as "most likable" in the yearbook. Class vice-president, homecoming king, object of feminine desire, Tommy made friends in all high school groups.

"Now the Carters lived in the shoe factory addition, a neighborhood a little less prosperous, perhaps, than others. One summer I was taking apart my bicycle's drive assembly, cleaning it, putting it back together with fresh grease, when Tommy came biking by."

Once more, many nods from the boys. Curtis recalled performing the same maintenance on his bike once a year. The operation was simple but necessary, as the mechanism wasn't permanently lubricated and sealed like those on later bikes.

Steve went on. "We all had one-speed bikes with pedal breaks, heavy, durable, though they were susceptible to rust. Letting them get wet and not drying them off was, my father insisted, a sign of faulty character."

Curtis remembered his own father's strict instructions to get his bike in the garage every night and any time it was raining. If he neglected it, he'd have to replace it with his own money.

"Tommy stopped to commend my efforts, and in the ensuing conversations about bike repair, changing tires, using flashlights for headlights we kind of got to know each other. And at the end, he invited me to go with him to help decorate a float for the Fourth of July parade."

This was an annual Fairfield event, as civic groups, churches, and clubs joined in to celebrate the local and the national community. Curtis had been a spectator for many years but was never involved as a participant.

I learned," concluded Steve, "that my father was right, of course, in one way. No human institution is perfect. But his argument left out other truths, too. Take the Lutheran church's parade float, which I did end up contributing to; it did have its flaws. The main problem involved Uncle Sam's ability to keep his head."

Beth whispered something to Sonja, and they both giggled. Curtis had noticed that their two heads were often close together in the course of the evening's events. It was more evidence for him that Southerners, or at least those who saw themselves in the New South, were often more relaxed than others with different races and in discussions of racial issues.

"Tommy was given the task of stabilizing Uncle Sam's wobbly head. And since I was with him, I became a partner in the process. Because the skeleton was already covered with chicken wire and stuffed with colored tissue paper, it was hard to make changes without destroying the face and the hat."

Mid leaned over toward Janet and said softly, "Do I hear a political allegory here?"

Janet whispered back. "The '60s were a time of challenges to the old order, that's for sure—a wobbly republic, according to some."

Curtis wagged a finger. "You two pipe down and let the man speak."

Steve explained. "What we needed was an artist and a eccentric bystander. And they both came forward. First, Tricia Bell!"

He smiled and pointed. She called out, "Drumsticks!"

"That's right. She had extra drumsticks," admitted Steve. "And the three of us realized we could brace Sam's neck using them as splints. But you know what was missing? In fact, not yet even invented."

"Duct tape!" called out a number of voices.

Exactly," said. "So who in a parade crowd would have a pre-duct tape duct tape."

A chorus erupted, "Bill Castle!"

Steve laughed. "Of course! As we all know, he didn't care about being stylish, and when the soles of his penny loafers began to separate from the tops with age, he just taped them in place with some electrician's tape. We laughed at him, but he just laughed back. That was the time, as I remember, he was, doing some kind of survey or study or . . . making a map!"

More laughter. And, when Steve pointed, heads turned to see Bill Castle waving from the doorway to the hall.

"So," concluded Steve, "the float problem was solved by committee, each member with a skill or a material that, when joined with the others, produced a solution. And that's when I saw a solution to another problem: my being a loner."

This time there was no confirmation. Rather, puzzled looks characterized the group.

"You see, when a community exists—and takes in a loner—they can make canoe paddles, airplane propellers, float figure support structures . . . whatever, by working together. And at the same time you build your faith in the human community, your belief in the possibility, as I see it, of the kingdom of God on earth."

He raised his glass. "To our class and its union of eccentrics. The room exploded with applause, raised glasses, and cheers.

Chapter Forty: Walks

In a final drive with Beth around the town's old neighborhoods Curtis realized he'd forgotten an interesting facet of town geography. Fairfield had forgotten it , too, as what he was recalling had disappeared.

"Right there," he told his wife, pointing. "That was where we used to walk to elementary school, before, that is, we moved to the Circle."

They were on the southeast side of town; the Circle was on the southwest.

"There?" Beth asked. "I just see houses. Did you cut through yards?"

"From what you see now, it's a logical conclusion. There's no way from here to Cedar Street. In fact, it looks as if most of these yards are fenced in. But there used to be a rock or gravel path—I'm not sure which, but not dirt—that went between these two homes, crossed the little creek in back over a wooden bridge, and ended up at a street on the other side."

If she'd been with them, his mother could have confirmed the streets and the pathway, but she'd already begun the trip with Carol up to John's house in St. Louis. They were all scheduled to fly home the next day—Mid, Curtis, and Beth to the East Coast; Carol and Mark to the West. The family would be spread out again just as the Fairfield High School class was now dispersing to other towns in the state and other states in the union.

"The bridge was really just some railroad ties bunched together," Curtis explained. "Solid enough if not especially attractive. And it was probably crossing more a ditch than a creek. Carol wasn't in school yet, but John and I hiked up and back to East Elementary every weekday."

"Go over to Cedar. Maybe it's visible on that side," suggested Beth.

They had driven up a semi-circular drive off an east-west state road that had marked the southern edge of Fairfield as Route 66 had once marked the northern. Curtis was a bit surprised at Beth's interest. She'd been here many times when his parents were alive and showed no particular desire to know the details of the town's layout.

"Fairfield Gardens," Curtis observed, "was what this neighborhood was called, and it was one of two U-shaped street loops off the highway with small houses on both sides—perhaps twenty in all. And there were smaller U-shaped loops branching off the large one, forming smaller neighborhoods of half a dozen homes. There, that's one up that lane."

Beth noted, "So, it's a web of connected developments—built during and after the war?"

"Right. Fort Leonard Wood, thirty miles away, grew a lot in those years, and there wasn't enough housing on base. Plus, the two geological surveys, state and national, were located here. They attracted new families in the '50s."

The Circle was another area where young families found affordable homes, their children becoming the baby boomers who now had and used their political power through such organizations as AARP.

"Before I turn back to Cedar," Curtis said, "let's look across the road." He drove out to the highway and then went east, remembering to the Green Acres development on the south side.

He found it immediately, surprised that he hadn't thought about these places in years. The new house his parents moved to when he was in college was along another semicircle drive off the same highway; it was modeled on the older neighborhoods but with larger lots and houses, a prosperous extension in the '60s and '70s following the 1950's layout.

As they rode slowly around Green Acres, Beth asked, "It was safe for children to walk from here all the way to school, to elementary school?"

"Well, kids over here had to get across the highway. I vaguely remember there being a crosswalk up by a grocery store down at Cedar Street. Maybe they used that. But the rest of us thought nothing about our daily trek."

Beth mused, "I'm guessing not everyone had two cars in those days, and walking was safe even for small children. It made sense for fathers to make paths like the one you described and create a passenger network joining different parts of town."

"Right. We had only one car until John was old enough to drive. Hmm, there was another similar area to the north of Fairfield Gardens, now that I think of it, but I can't recall the name. Tim Carlson lived there; I'll have to ask him—or Wild Bill. But I bet there were cut throughs all over the place."

"What makes me curious about this was what Sonja, your classmate, told me about her experience."

"Uh-oh," admitted Curtis. "This might not reflect well on local attitudes at the time."

They had come back past Fairfield Gardens and turned up Cedar Street. The site of his old elementary school was half a mile to the north.

Beth asked, "Wasn't the black school, Lincoln, in this area?"

The questions surprised Curtis. "You're right. Just two blocks over and maybe one up. Since I didn't know what it was when I got older, I saw it only as a church. Wow, I'm not seeing a new town here but an old one some of whose features I had overlooked."

"That's what Sonja told me. She lived on Second Street, not too far from the Circle."

"I remember that area. It's just four or five blocks west of where we are, this side of the highway from the Circle. We walked or biked through there on the way to town or to school, but I don't recall any African American families there." He sighed. "So, again, they must have simply not registered in my consciousness."

"Drive over there," Beth said. "I want to see. Sonja told me how kids she was in classes and in clubs with would pass through her neighborhood and not even recognize her. When she called out to them, most ducked their heads, mumbled some vague response, and walked faster."

"It seems, though, she at least was able to take advantage of our school academically, going on to achieve so much in her career."

"I think she was probably an exception. She told me she had extra motivation because her older brother, ten years her senior, had to attend the Lincoln School but then dropped out at ninth grade. The family had no way to get him to Jefferson City, where there was a black school he could have attended."

Curtis remembered all he's learned from Abraham and Jefferson. And again, he realized that the framework within which he had seen his past was inadequate. At least in his research for the yearbook, and in his experience with his own children's schools in Virginia, he had fashioned a better one. Sonja's story, though, showed that he would probably continue to correct his pictures of the past.

He recalled once more the high school band's visit to Hermann, Missouri, and the tour of a mushroom factory built into the side of hill—thus, essentially invisible. Curtis had been surprised to hear the workers speaking another language.

That they were probably from Mexico didn't occur to Curtis until now, when so much agricultural labor in this country is handled by immigrants, documented and not. He hadn't thought they traveled outside of California, Arizona, and New Mexico. But apparently, they stayed out of view in Missouri—like the mushrooms they were growing.

He drove through the area Sonja had lived in, which lay between his old neighborhood of the Circle and downtown. He remembered small homes on irregular lots, back- and side-yard vegetable and flower gardens, laundry clothes lines.

He remembered a back way out to Main Street, old Route 66, which became Business Route 66, then simply Main Street as the first by-pass went on the western edge of town and later when the four-lane Interstate 44 ran north of Fairfield.

He told Beth, "You see the 'Historic Route 66' everywhere along the old road in its various manifestations over the years.

I'm told there are some stretches of the highway, though, not identified because enthusiasts might come and chip out a chunk as a souvenir. The true cognizant don't want those pieces to disappear completely."

"So, the complete Mother Road is still be discovered," said Beth, " I'm glad that you brought the Lincoln School back to life, as it were, though this reunion and *Confluence II*. Perhaps other efforts will recover Sonja's presence in her old neighborhood as well as in Malaysia and the Philippines where she served her country very well."

Curtis sighed. "For all I know, Bill's idea of a Cherokee population in town will also have to be acknowledged." He signed again. "I wanted to recall some good times from the past—Bridge Déjà Vu —but I've come to realize the portrait has to be modified to acknowledge a broader reality. Could there be *Confluence III*?"

Epilogue: Mid-

Curtis found the following letter among his mother's papers after she passed. She was two weeks short of her 101st birthday.

* * * *

When Curtis first proposed I accompany him to his high school class's 50th reunion, I was less concerned than I thought I would be, given my health. Even though I'd had a fall and was using a walker in rehab, I was intrigued by the idea of one final trip.

Curtis was convinced I would regain the full (if senior) strength of my legs; but my doctors told me the hip wouldn't be restored without surgery. And my heart being the way it was, it was unlikely I could survive an operation. So, I went, and I came back.

Five years before that, on my 95th birthday, I had begun to compose, with Curtis's help, a family chronicle that reached a nice conclusion with 100th birthday and the return to Fairfield. But that does not mean finality, however, as, once born, we are always in middles of ongoing, connected events.

The physical details of human birth were so hidden in the 1950s that, when my son referred in a high school class to a twin's emergence from a mother's womb—claiming the title of the first born ahead (literally) of a second child—the teacher had to change the topic quickly. Don't look there!

My husband Oscar tended not to look there, true to his Scandinavian heritage, his religious upbringing, and his love of the ideal. I, however, remain intrigued and frankly thrilled to wonder what remains to be seen the closer we look at our bodies—into cells, chromosomes, DNA—and the father away we view the vastness but not emptiness of space.

My nickname growing up was 'Mid." I was the middle sister of three and the middle child of five. I grew up thinking that a nickname of "Mid" was bad, that being in the middle meant I was lost, unnoticed, insignificant. I have come see that to be "mid-"—a midpoint between extreme positions or opinions—is not bad. To be "mid-" also suggests being at some point in a process, which, in fact, we always are. One generation succeeds another just as one story takes a next place in literary history.

This linear/temporal movement occurs in the physical world. Historic Route 66 has taken the place of the Mother Road (wherever pavement still exists in a changing landscape) and still stretches "from Chicago to L.A.," as the song says. My son's friends completed their four years of high school fifty years ago, but a new crop of achievers has marched across the same (though renovated) stage to begin their adult journeys. (Two received handsome scholarships, thanks to their fellow students from long ago.)

For a century I've watched loved ones at home and watched them go away to engage in the struggles of distant lands. What holds a people together has been strained perhaps to a breaking point by the ease of modern travel, the power of scientific and technological development, the range of opportunity. Though I don't understand exactly why, I still have faith that the human community will survive no matter how far apart we drift or how many conflicts plague us.

Still, it's true that, before I was one year old, a first world war began. It was supposed to "end all wars," but a second came soon after I turned thirty. And then my children's experience in Vietnam and in the Middle East added to the history of combat. We, as a nation, seem right now to be in a time of (relative) peace, but I can spin a globe and point to half a dozen sites where potential antagonism can move from being latent to viral and draw us in.

To assert the ongoing nature of our existence, I must at the outset acknowledge divisions, some of which generate conflict.

My childhood was divided into summers on Greenwood Lake in northern New Jersey and winters in Rutherford, across the Hudson River from Manhattan. My father, who'd grown up on a farm before coming to New York City to make his fortune, was never completely happy in an urban setting. So, he bought a small piece of land on the lake and built a campsite, later added a tent, and finally constructed a primitive cabin. The five children and Mother were there every day from early June to late August.

Mother, I would eventually learn, would not have chosen this division of the school year and the summer. She was a city person, a poet, a thinker who struggled with domestic chores. While we dreaded the return to school, she welcomed it.

Father could not spend his entire summer at the lake. Every Monday morning he would take a ferry to the opposite shore, where he boarded a train into the city. He reversed the journey on Friday. Holidays like the Fourth of July, of course, extended his stays at the lake.

Today, that man's grandson—my son Curtis—lives on a stretch of a North Carolina river about the same size as Greenwood Lake. Although my official residence is a retirement home fifteen miles away, I spend many days there, often staying nights in a downstairs bedroom with a view of the water. To be honest, I'd like that to be the place where I peacefully take my last breath, a breath that connects to those of my earliest years.

The sharpest mental image I have of my father at Greenwood Lake is his morning swim, his head upright always, an unlit beacon of his enjoyment of life and nature.

With brothers and sisters, I also swam, climbed the hills behind our campsite, hiked to our few and distant neighbors. We would read, draw, sing with no regular schedule or duties other than helping to keep the campsite clean and to prepare meals. It was an ideal child's life.

I've learned that this was a life of privilege, available to me as a product of a prosperous country, hardworking parents, and an unrecognized class system that protected us from those who might envy our comfort. We all want such joy for our children, of course; but while common in our literary tradition, such a carefree outdoor childhood is rare in the larger world where poverty and sickness constrain human happiness.

At the midpoint of my years in Fairfield, I pursued the possibility of a place on the water in central Missouri. Another of the state's small rivers was being dammed to make a lake—smaller than the Lake of the Ozarks, but with a similar prospect of summer cottages and recreation. I saw a flyer about it in the county courthouse and insisted Oscar come look at a plot.

The county courthouse where I saw the flyer was (and is) an imposing two-story, red Greek Revival style brick building constructed in the 1860s. The structure would have been about 100 years old and Fairfield a few years older when I took up the idea of a water home.

The town in which I spent more than half a century (and thus half my life) had been in 1860 at the end of the southwest branch of the Pacific Railroad, and thus a strategic location in the American Civil War. The courthouse became a Union hospital at that time.

If I came into being as a world war was beginning and am likely to leave it before our longest war (in Afghanistan) ends, and as I have lived through more than half a dozen major conflicts my country played roles in, it might seem odd that I never mentioned in this chronicle this nation's Civil War and Fairfield's place in it.

Noted in history books as a border state, Missouri did not take a prominent role in my conception of the "War Between the States," which focused on major battles in Pennsylvania, Virginia, and Georgia. The area's role in the Civil War provided no guides for my children's military service. Still, here in what I believe to be a final installment of my own history, I will set foot in this tragedy of a nation divided, again to acknowledge that there are always divisions among us. Especially in marriage, there are two sides that struggle to reconcile.

I tend to be a down to earth person, someone who wants to put a hand on the topic at hand. Picture me, then, holding the hand of a man I have often characterized as a dreamer while poking a stick into one quarter of an acre of Missouri clay bordered by a small creek that, it was promised, would spread into a picturesque body of water. "We can afford it," I explained. "And it would be a fine project for our retirement."

He nodded and sheltered his pipe against a slight breeze in order to relight it.

"Let's see," he began, once the tobacco was burning and he could draw smoke in and blow it out. "It took us about 43 minutes to drive the 37 miles up here. And, of course, the return would involve the same time and gas, so we would have to subtract approximately an hour and half—plus travel costs from our, um, from our enjoyment of each visit to a second home."

I knew immediately that this was the end of the discussion. His calculations of time and space would expand, a sign that, while the idea might appeal to him as an interesting problem to study, he would be drawn into an endless consideration of possibility and probability, not the purchase of a plot or the construction of a building.

I'd known his attraction to the abstract when I fell in love with him and understood that my late-life water home would remain a dream. But as I've said, it has materialized—been reborn—in the mind and the landscape of his son. That re-birth overcomes finality, as I said at the beginning.

Onward, then, family and friends, together.

———————————

Enjoy this excerpt from another in Michael Lund's Open Book, Open Road Novel Series, *Route 66 Sweetheart.*

Volume One: Indoors and Out

Chapter One: Here I Am!

To Marian, growing up in northeastern New Jersey just across the Hudson River from New York City, the important things in life seemed either very far away or almost too close. What mattered was out of reach or suffocating. She could find little middle ground. Marian's father had not been sent "over there" during World War I because she and her two older siblings, John and Ella, had been born by 1917. But Curtis was profoundly affected by that historic conflict. And he was away from home frequently during the years his children were growing up (in addition to Marian, there would be two more, Alice and Bill).

Curtis Lacy rode the train to work in Manhattan every weekday. And, as a marine insurance adjustor, he often traveled to coastal and river cities throughout the country. A few times he went overseas for months at a time. So, one of the most consistent images of Marian's childhood was the figure of her father disappearing down Ridge Road as he strode briskly toward the train station in early morning light. Away.

Mid's two sisters and two brothers, on the other hand, were so close at home they often seemed to stifle her. Not that she didn't love them (and the two grandparents who had lived with them in their widowhood), but if she'd had her own room (rather than sharing with Ella and Alice), or if she'd had some secret hideout like Judy Bolton in her favorite children's stories, she felt she could have maintained a better balance in her day-to-day affairs. Her mother seldom left the house or its flower garden, but she often seemed distant. Marian assumed this was because Mrs. Ethel Lacy was thinking of grown-up things children would not understand. What her mother was contemplating would become clear only years later, however, at the time of her father's unexpected death.

The middle Lacy child also couldn't know for more than a decade that the man who would become the father of her children was half a continent away, moving with his carpenter father and schoolteacher mother from job to job in a Midwest hard hit by the Depression. They would not live in the same city until well after Marian's sense that she had either to get away from a crowded house or find a retreat deeper within it was made most distinct one summer day in the 1930s.

Her older brother, John, was a student at M.I.T, coming home only on occasional weekends. The next in age, Ella, considered the family beauty, was being courted by high school classmates and a few college men, so the three younger siblings often played together in the evenings. While Marian, Alice, and Bill were having a three-handed cribbage tournament, their mother was sitting on the sofa organizing family pictures into a new album. "Mother?" Mid asked. "What's that?"

The question was, she thought, rhetorical. Every time her mother arranged photos the topic of Ethel's lost brother surfaced. And she would tear up. "It's Uncle Henry, isn't it?" Alice whispered to Marian.

"Muggins!" exclaimed Bill. Alice had failed to count his nobs, but it wasn't clear that she'd finished totaling her score. Marian intervened, putting a hand on Bill's shoulder and pulling him toward her.

"That's not fair; we were talking to Mother. Mother, what is that picture?"

Ethel did have her characteristic faraway look, and her eyes were moist. Marian assumed she was thinking of Henry, their uncle who had disappeared more than a dozen years earlier. A bachelor at thirty-five, he'd gone on a business trip to Canada and never returned. There were stories in the papers of a train wreck outside Toronto, and the family came to believe he must have been aboard. But the fact that nothing could be confirmed inspired a number of stories.

"No, Alice. It's not my brother." Like most mothers, she could somehow understand her children's whispering. "It's about Mid," she explained.

"Me? Let me see."

All three climbed up from the rug, Bill trying to push past Alice. "That's not a picture," he noted.

"It's a poem, a poem about your sister."

"Let us read it!" commanded Alice.

But Ethel tucked the folded paper back into the album. "Let me tell you about it instead." She pulled Bill close. The sisters settled themselves on two wingback chairs. "You were too young to remember, but one summer Marian got very, very sick."

"That time I had the flu?"

"Yes. At least, that's what we thought it was. Then Dr. Paterson did this test--a blood test of some kind, I think. Two days later he gave us bad news: leukemia."

Alice gasped. "You die from that!"

"Yes, you do. There was no treatment for it then, and there's none now either."

"The test must have been wrong," said Bill. "Here she is!"

"Here I am, yes," mused Marian. This year in biology class she had been introduced to a microscope. She would use many more in her ten-year career as a medical technologist, finding and drawing such tiny creatures that--though less than a foot from her careful eye--they seemed to exist in another, faraway universe. She imagined Dr. Paterson studying her blood, finding oddly shaped cells, a sign of destiny.

"I remember that summer. We were getting ready to go to the lake when I got so sick I couldn't get out of bed."

The family had a campsite on Greenwood Lake where they stayed from early summer until school began again in the fall, though Curtis had to commute into the city every weekday.

"Not so many had flu that year, not like it had been in 1918 or '19, but you were just as ill."

"I remember the war was over, though there were ever so many wounded and sick soldiers. Anyway, I do know that Doctor Paterson said I had to rest. I went to bed, and you put away all our camping equipment."

"It was weeks before you were well. We were never sure what your condition was, though it couldn't have been leukemia. And we even went to the lake after all. We got there just in time for Fourth of July. What a celebration! Fireworks over the water, and . . . "

"And?"

"Well, Dr. Paterson came to visit our campsite. It was just two tents back then. But the doctor brought me a present. Or perhaps it was for Father. They were fast friends."

"A keepsake?"

"You could say that--the poem." She patted the album. "He wrote a lot of poems. They tell me he's become pretty well known, especially in Europe. But I never could understand them. The things he wrote were just . . . sort of like snapshots, a picture of some scene."

"Was the poem about Mid, then?" asked Alice.

It told about the whole family, our going to the lake. In the poem a little child is sick, and then she seems to die and rise up as some kind of angel."

"She doesn't act like an angel now," argued Bill.

Their mother laughed. "No, but neither do you, young man. Now, back to your game. I've got things to do in the kitchen."

She rose, taking the album with her. Sensing finality in this statement, Marian herded her younger siblings back to the rug, and the game resumed. But as she played, she tried to imagine the poem's words. She pictured herself as the child in the poem, an indistinct figure kept at a distance for some reason by her mother. It was a shadowy figure, a ghost of a girl perhaps.

When she'd been sick, she'd drifted in and out of dreams, rising and falling from restless sleep. The real world had seemed far away then--her older brother and sister at play in another room, neighbors strolling past on a Sunday afternoon, distant trains rolling north and south. She didn't know where she was or where she was supposed to be. She had trouble putting it into words, but her mother's withdrawal also left Mid drifting. At times she felt cut off from both parents.

Had Ethel Lacy been changed by the scare of that summer? Who had she been before she married Curtis and began to have children? Was there more to the story of her uncle's

235

disappearance? How did Mid fit into this family history? The four-year-old Mid, sick in bed, was now far away from the teenaged Marian, more like another person than herself at an earlier age. In a sense, Mid realized, that child had died.

Once recovered and coming home from the lake, Marian had felt different, wise in some way children were not supposed to be and sad about the gap in her existence, the period of illness. The girl in the poem--who was she? Marian before she got sick? The self she had become at age seventeen? An entirely different person she must still bring into being? At that moment she realized that her true self could be in the future, away and beckoning. She would have to search for that woman, outside this house or inside her imagination. She could begin tomorrow.   . . . to be continued.

OPEN Road
OPEN Book
Novel Series

Michael Lund's five-volume novel series chronicles an American family during times of peace and war from 1915 to 2015.

Route 66 Déjà Vu explores the confirmations and revisions of individual and collective history for a generation that grew up in the '50s and '60s in a small town on The Mother Road. The occasions are a 50th high school class reunion and the 100th birthday of one classmate's mother, the matriarch of her family and a representative of the Greatest Generation. The stories of the class' male and female Vietnam veterans are integrated into the longer narrative and present a distinctive perspective on the American Dream.

Route 66 Sweetheart tells the story of a young woman growing up in Rutherford, New Jersey, in the 1930s. Marion (Mid) Lacy traces her ancestry back to the early New World Settlement of Nantucket and will become the matriarch of a Midwestern family. As a young woman, though, her dreams of the future overshadowed by more brilliant siblings and friends. In an era of hard times haunted by the prospect of approaching world war, she learns that all are counted in the creation of history.

Route 66 Dreamer features Oscar Lindbloom, the son of a Swedish immigrant and an Ozark farm woman who pursues his dreams of American success in Kansas and Missouri in the early 1940s. A romantic and a scientist at the same time, he falls in love (long distance) with Marian Lacy, a native of New Jersey, the couple becoming part of the World War II Generation who build post-war America.

In *Route 66 Looking-glass* Mid (Lacy) Lindbloom and husband Oscar—with grown children (mostly) on their own—assess their life's successes and plans for the future. The mid-1960's is a time of turmoil for the nation, though, and they worry that the American definition of success has been constricted to material prosperity. The dream of "the Mother Road" appears illusory when reflected against the realities of injustice in the nation and of war abroad.

Farewell, Route 66 begins on the eve of the first Gulf War as seventeen members of the Lindbloom family gather for Christmas in St. Louis on the decommissioned national highway Route 66. Can the family and the nation survive the new forces that will shape the 21st-century? The younger generation question the conventions of their parents and travel to Europe and the Middle East to understand their identity in a multi-national community.

About the Author

Dr. Michael Lund, Professor Emeritus of English at Longwood University, is a native of Rolla, Missouri, and lives in Virginia with his wife of 55 years. Their two grown children are gifted educators.

In addition to having published scholarly books and articles about 19th- and 20th-century British and American literature, he is the author of novels inspired by Route 66, America's Mother Road. He has also produced two collections of short stories: *How to Not Tell a War Story* (2012) and *Eating With Veterans* (2015). He currently is working on a novel series set in a small coastal Carolina village.

Lund also directs Home and Abroad, a free writing program for military, veterans, and family, in rural central Virginia. He was a U.S. Army correspondent at Fort Campbell, Kentucky (1969-70) and in Vietnam (1970-71). Several dozen of his recent short stories reflecting military experience have appeared in contemporary journals, including "Left-Hearted," *Line of Advance* (2016); reprinted in *Our Best War Stories: An Anthology of Darron L. Wright Award Winners.* Middle West Press (October 2020).

The author may be contacted:
https://homeandabroadva.com/

Scan QR Code to go to the website.

Made in the USA
Middletown, DE
05 November 2023

41821814R00142